Brilliance Is the Clothing I Wear

Brilliance Is the Clothing Is I Wear

NEW WRITING FROM
INKWELL WORKSHOPS
VOLUME 4

INTRODUCTION BY **ROXANNA BENNETT**

DUNDURN
PRESS

"Father" and "In Observance of My Loneliness" by George Zancola first published in the *Humber Literary Review*.

Publisher: Scott Fraser
Editorial Committee: Maya Ameyaw, Leonarda Carranza, Eunice Cu, Kathy Friedman, Yasaman Mansoori, Joseph Pirrello | Editor: Kathy Friedman
Copy Editor: Stuart Ross | Designer: Rudi Garcia
Cover image: Apanaki Temitayo M
Sponsors:

 Canadian Mental Health Association Toronto

Library and Archives Canada Cataloguing in Publication

Title: Brilliance is the clothing I wear.
Description: Series statement: New writing from InkWell Workshops ; volume 4
Identifiers: Canadiana (print) 20210160632 | Canadiana (ebook) 20210160799 | ISBN 9781459747708 (softcover) | ISBN 9781459747715 (PDF) | ISBN 9781459747722 (EPUB)
Subjects: CSH: Mentally ill, Writings of the, Canadian (English)—Ontario—Toronto. | CSH: Recovering addicts' writings, Canadian (English)—Ontario—Toronto. | CSH: Canadian literature (English)—Ontario—Toronto. | CSH: Canadian literature (English)—21st century.
Classification: LCC PS8235.M45 B75 2021 | DDC C810.8/092074—dc23

  Canada Council for the Arts Conseil des arts du Canada   Ontario

 ONTARIO ARTS COUNCIL CONSEIL DES ARTS DE L'ONTARIO an Ontario government agency un organisme du gouvernement de l'Ontario  ONTARIO CREATES

We acknowledge the support of the Canada Council for the Arts and the Ontario Arts Council for our publishing program. We also acknowledge the financial support of the Government of Ontario, through the Ontario Book Publishing Tax Credit and Ontario Creates, and the Government of Canada.

Care has been taken to trace the ownership of copyright material used in this book. The author and the publisher welcome any information enabling them to rectify any references or credits in subsequent editions.

The publisher is not responsible for websites or their content unless they are owned by the publisher.

Dundurn Press
1382 Queen Street East
Toronto, Ontario, Canada M4L 1C9
dundurn.com, @dundurnpress 🐦 f 📷

CONTENTS

Introduction 1
ROXANNA BENNETT

Chinese Food with David (memoir) 6
REBECCA CHERNECKI

Vestiges of Love (poem) 8
REBECCA CHERNECKI

A Lazy Day (poem) 10
JOSEPH PIRRELLO

Restless Soul (memoir) 11
JOSEPH PIRRELLO

Father (poem) 12
GEORGE ZANCOLA

In Observance of My Loneliness (poem) 14
GEORGE ZANCOLA

The Destination Rhyme (poem) 16
GEORGE ZANCOLA

The Ribfest Psychic (fiction) 18
HOWARD J. SANCHEZ

Memories of Dawn (poem) 24
MARK HARVEY

Blunting the Edges of Nostalgia (poem) 25
FATHUMA JAMA

Blueberry Imprints (memoir) 26
EUNICE CU

A Life in Ten (poem) 32
MG SHEPHERD

Wilson Avenue (poem) 33
DANA SAHADATH

Blood Orange (memoir) 34
YASAMAN MANSOORI

Enjoy Your Morning Brew, Nice and Slow! (poem) 36
ASPI KOOTAR

Skeleton Coaster (poem) 37
ASUKA LAPIERRE

Despondent (poem) 38
MICHELE BRETON

Fragments (poem) 39
ADAM ZABOROWSKI

The Taste of Home (fiction) 40
NORIKO HOSHINO

The Red Blanket (fiction) 50
JAMES WAGSTAFF

How to Make a Stir-Fry (poem) 54
PAMELA CHYNN

The Mango (poem) 56
PAMELA CHYNN

Abstractions (poem) 57
HONEY NOVICK

What All the Rage Is (poem) 59
LORETTA FISHER

Zaya (fiction) 61
KOSHALA NALLANAYAGAM

Invasive Species (fiction) 65
DONNA COOKE

Agape (poem) 68
DANIELA VIOLIN

The Damn Poem (poem) 69
LAUREL SCHELL

Ten Things I Learned About Angela (poem) 73
PUJA MALANI

Travelling 101 (memoir) 74
SHEREL PURCELL

Excerpts from Kismet *(fiction)* 80
MAYA AMEYAW

Coming Home from Death —
Meeting Life with Spirit (memoir) 83
ROMAINE JONES

Dying (poem) 86
EMILY GILLESPIE

Library Script (poem) 87
EMILY GILLESPIE

The Cover Artist 91

About the Contributors 92

INTRODUCTION

ROXANNA BENNETT

It's winter as I attempt to write this, a challenging season for many people, even without the pandemic. The holidays, a source of triggering pain and suicidal ideation, are finally over, thank every deity. I personally have many unpleasant anniversaries close to the holidays that make navigating the season a minefield. Grief so deep I can't breathe. It's hard to get up off the floor. The sky is a migraine and I'll never feel warm again. I weigh a thousand pounds and can't remember laughter.

But then I read something like this and remember why I agreed to write this introduction:

> "—on my battered coffee table is a volume on mad people's history showing me I'm not the only one who's been cast out of society and viewed as useless, reminding me that my life is shaped by trends in psychiatric treatment. Mad people's history whispers to me: it's okay, you have a right to be here, please stay a little longer, for those of us who didn't make it..." (Emily Gillespie, "Library Script")

It's okay. You have a right to be here. Please stay a little longer. I whisper these words to myself over and over as I struggle to focus, to open my laptop and sit down to write words I feel singularly unqualified to write. They're much nicer than the words running through my head on a perpetual loop: *You're so stupid and lazy, you'll never finish this introduction, you're an uneducated fraud, you're going to screw this up just like you screw up everything else.*

We navigate this world through narrative; it's how we understand ourselves and others. We don't often experience words of kindness if we are Mad, insane, neurodivergent, neuroatypical, brain-disordered, brain different, traumatized, manic, depressed, anxious, panicked, psychotic. Most mentally ill people are living at the edges of human contact.

Doctors, psychiatrists, social workers, the people who ostensibly care for the mentally ill, don't have time or space for compassionate connection or attentive, non-judgmental listening. There isn't a sense of shared humanity so much as the sensation of acting out a script you're all forced to perform, as patient client or doctor caregiver. No psychiatrist, no nurse, however well-meaning, has ever looked me in the face and said, *It's okay. You have a right to be here. Please stay a little longer.*

One of the many lessons of the pandemic is how deeply we need each other, and that not one of us is truly alone. Without the hard work of strangers, the people who put the toothpaste in the tubes, stock the grocery-store shelves, grow and pick the food, the people who make and fill my prescriptions, the hundreds and thousands of people, I would not exist. And without drop-in programs for people with mental illness, I would also not be here to struggle to write this introduction. More than a physical space, the very concept of a drop-in, a free non-judgmental space run by people who also have a hard time being alive, is a lifesaver.

When I have been on the edge of a subway platform daring myself to jump, when I have been friendless, penniless, hopeless, desperately alone, I have always had a tiny sliver of possibility, knowing that drop-in programs exist. That it was possible to find my way to a group of people who had also struggled and suffered.

It's okay. You have a right to be here. Please stay a little longer.

Shared vulnerabilities enrich human connection and deepen our understanding of what it is to be a person in this world. In guiding people to tell their stories through their own lens, in their own voice, without judgment or censure, InkWell gifts us new vocabularies and ways of being. A cognitive behavioural therapy worksheet and a prescription will never heal the human heart the same way as sharing your unique perspective with other human beings who have also experienced unrelenting pain being alive.

On days when I feel alienated, isolated, and alone, it helps to know there are other artists who share these experiences with each other and the world, through anthologies like this one. As an artist navigating the mental health system, my claim to be a poet was seen as a symptom, a delusion of grandeur, my inability to recite my work on demand by psychiatrists was taken as further evidence of my delusion. I took to carrying a copy of my book with me to all intake appointments so I could prove to the doctors that I wasn't lying. So it brings me tremendous joy to be a part of this anthology, to know that these contributors have been supported and believed as creative people and that through their art they have had the opportunity to express their uniqueness to the world.

Any book is evidence of a team of people labouring to make it a tangible object, but an anthology takes a community to create. In addition to the twenty-eight contributors whose work you will find in these pages, this book was brought into being by an editorial committee made up of InkWell staff and participants: Kathy Friedman, Leonarda Carranza, Maya Ameyaw, Joseph Pirrello, Eunice Cu, and Yasaman Mansoori, who received and reviewed submissions from thirty-seven InkWell participants. Kathy Friedman edited the anthology, and the poet Stuart Ross copy-edited it. The Reva Gerstein Legacy Fund will pay the contributors. The cover art, a gorgeous piece by Apanaki Temitayo M, was chosen from a contest for visual artists with lived experience. Dundurn Press will design, print, and distribute the book. And the readers who will find the work will carry it further; all are welcome at the drop-in.

Brilliance Is the Clothing I Wear is a work of love, devotion, dedication, compassion, and the ability to embrace people in all of their complexities. In all of their—as Honey Novick writes in her poem "Abstractions," from which this collection takes its name—"imperfections and sensitivities."

．．．．．．．．．．．．．．

> Brilliance is the clothing I wear
> to gingerly open the door of my vulnerabilities
> those imperfections and sensitivities
> as I point to the love I seek to protect.

The authors of the pieces collected in this anthology are clad in brilliance. Their work is a doorway pointing toward a more authentic way of being than the daily world most people consider "normal." Through their collective vulnerabilities and sensitivities, they seek to guide and welcome us into a community of bravery and battered hearts.

To be mentally ill is to have the ability to admit that life is difficult and painful—sometimes, often, overwhelmingly so. We're taught to tough everything out alone, to internalize our struggles and sorrows, we're taught that emotions are inconvenient and messy and ugly and certainly not to be shown or shared. To be mentally ill is to know that all of that is farcical. Sharing our struggles and sorrows is exactly what saves us, what carries us home to ourselves. To be mentally ill is to know that everyone has their own reality, demons, angels, ways of being, and that it's okay to share space with each other, even and especially through our differences.

It's okay. You have a right to be here. Please stay a little longer.

I invite you to *gingerly open the door of your vulnerabilities* as you read this collection. The pandemic has taught us how interconnected we all are, how we depend upon one another for everything: food, shelter, medicine, love, each other. These are our essentials. The most important service we can provide for each other is our presence, showing up for each other non-judgmentally, in support and empathy. We are all alike in our desire to be free of suffering. And we can alleviate the great suffering in this world by listening to each other, open-heartedly, unreservedly, by trying to hear ourselves inside each other's stories.

．．．．．．．．．．．．．

In this anthology, you will find work about family, loss, community, adventure, companionship, love, the search for justice and meaning. You will find work that makes you laugh, that confounds you, that moves you, confuses you, frightens you. You will find invitations to share a cup of coffee, a chat, a moment, a breath of meaning, of true connection. You will find yourself reflected, invited, and reassured.

It's okay. You have a right to be here. Please stay a little longer.

Roxanna Bennett
January 10, 2021

CHINESE FOOD WITH DAVID

REBECCA CHERNECKI

I was always happy when David suggested we order in Chinese food. It was kind of romantic, and I loved how it was "our thing" to do, when we could leave our troubles behind and just eat.

Sometimes he paid for it, bless his heart. I didn't always have the money. The food was so abundant, it made me feel like I was in Heaven. His healthy appetite almost startled me; he ate heartily, and with a grace and countenance that expressed real gratitude.

That's what I loved most about him—he always seemed so grateful for his lot. I, on the other hand, struggled to eat. I fluctuated between two states: feeling glory with all this food, then suddenly retreating in embarrassment that I actually had an appetite at all.

My eating disorder was quite pronounced in those days. Years ago, my sister had humiliated me in front of the whole family at an Italian restaurant. I was very hungry, and I announced to the table what I would be ordering. My sister looked at me and said flatly, "You are obese!"

I will never forget that day. She has also called me a hindrance and a failure, and she insists that I do nothing to help myself—that I stay in a rut, get in trouble with bad people, and don't care about my own life.

Anyway, David was full of a bountiful generosity, whereby I did not usually feel guilty about eating, did not hate myself for being hungry, did not feel remorse when I looked at him, and did not regret the $6.50 meal. It accented our sex life, as after eating, we both had energy and strength to make love while also feeling that we loved ourselves.

The peace in our relationship lasted for some time. Then my mother complained about the cost of Chinese food and said, "When you get a job, that's when you can entertain or eat takeout food."

Since then I have felt a permanent guilt about eating restaurant food. It's no wonder I am grumpy and lost—poverty zaps nearly all my strength. Whereas my sister eats exactly what she wants, when she wants, with whom she wants.

My starvation doesn't get noticed or addressed anymore. But when and if I eat Chinese food again, I'll remember David as a friend who loved my belly, breasts, and rotund arms. Even when I was hungry.

VESTIGES OF LOVE

REBECCA CHERNECKI

In the forest of my heart—green, leafy, fertile—
we kindle something lost to the Moon's fire,
orange and red. Electric currents of thought prevail
as I walk through Time, demarcated like sidewalks.
I long to stroll with you down a cobblestone road,
perhaps in Quebec City.

You are the boy I would have chosen as a girl of ten,
the one I would have written to, expressed my
brown tones and white bones to,
the one I would have embodied in my hair, whipping
through the wind, or I would have
taken the wild tiger lilies from my garden and painted
them for you, painted them for your wall.

Would you have been a poor man living alone
too old in your soul for love?
Or would I have been a crone
wearing silver hoops worn down
from carrying them in my jewellery box?
Or would I be the Mary Magdalene of your hopes,
anointing your temples from an alabaster jar
of essential oil of lavender, sinning
my breasts in your mouth as I
kissed you half-heartedly?

Once you visited.
Now we only speak. You
are a promise in the night,
an earthly movement that attracts my eyes
as you peer into the Heavens
for an answer.

A LAZY DAY

JOSEPH PIRRELLO

He lies in a field
Chewing on a blade of
Grass. The indolent clouds
Hover over the humming of the
Idyll oozing from the drifter's
Mouth. All is embedded in stillness;
All awaits a nudge from a bluesy
Breeze. The surrounding hills
As by telepathy exchange their woes;
Melancholy stiffens the stems
Of the hand-shaped leaves.
The stench of the dead swallow gives
The day its tone, and the animals graze
Slowly, as though their appetites had
Wings that take flight, leaving their bellies
Empty. A toad has not leapt for an hour;
The world is unconscious;
Nothing moves;
The sun, too, desecrates its routine,
Ignoring its descent.

RESTLESS SOUL

JOSEPH PIRRELLO

She paces the halls, trying to remember things. Only a few months ago she breezed through her chores with little effort, and even smiled when reminiscing about her childhood back in Sicily. Although her arranged marriage made her a bitter woman, she always found a way to alleviate sorrow. Now her thoughts stumble, and she can hardly recall what she did minutes earlier. How sad, the deterioration of a mind, sinking like a bombarded ship and slowly reaching the depths of total incoherence.

Ninety is quite the age. Ninety years of challenges that would have thwarted a mountain climber. Her summit is now out of reach. Every day presents a heavy load for an elderly woman who cannot even remember where she placed a piece of scrap paper, a note, or a shopping list. As she mines the field of what she can remember, she slips into melancholia, sobbing in silence while she knits in her chair, nestled in a den lined with ornaments. The thought of her mortality is a solace. She escapes despair by imagining herself lying in a quiet crypt, where no one and nothing can reach her. Frustrated, her grown children try to rouse her from her confused state; they quietly sob without letting their mother know that they, too, despair.

The wind outside speaks its own lethargic language. A flashback strikes the elderly woman, and for a few moments she remains still in her kitchen, stirring a pot of pasta and watching the boiling water. Cooking puts her in a gloomy trance. She's stirred pasta many times, but now it is toilsome. A nurse is needed to help her shower; this, too, is laborious. As the days pass and as the months pass also, her aging body aches, and she sighs with utter defeat. She retires in the evening, not knowing if the next day will arrive, and if it does, if it will present more of a struggle than the previous day. She wonders if the Almighty still has a hopeful itinerary for her days. She needs a favourable resolution to all her suffering, like a gust of fresh air, not whirling but gently stroking her pallid cheeks.

FATHER

GEORGE ZANCOLA

From the empty motive in his throat
to the fright he bore in the shadow of death,
my father ruled the earth.

An island stood in the middle
of his heart, and long boats moved through his veins,
each boat a shout, each shout a spear.

His redemption resided inside silk purses filled
with his peculiar visions of heaven.
His freedom came in gold and silver.

His being moved like a fat dancer
in the thunder and light of the howl of love
he found inside trenches of pain.

The old man was a trawler who fished
with a net of spines, eyes of wire dragging
his charges further into the sea of drowning.

He found his ideas in a deck of cards
he shuffled in triumph and rage,
his poverty clutched in his fist, his open hand holding

only colour and wind. The man's kingdom thrived
in sight, in sound, in air. His voice
was a scream in the cave of loneliness.

His love and kindness brokered his abysmal will.
In the genius of hatred, with a hammer of deceit,
his dark countenance boasted of trespass,

with laughter mad as torture. Greed
defined his holiness, and largesse
the miracle of his faith. He stood at the

front entrance of the world wanting peace,
and from his place of bones, from
the emptiness of denied truth, with words

thin and cruel, and his thought a distillation
of fact into fancy, he was the end of all things,
and the harsh and horrid beginning of everything.

IN OBSERVANCE OF MY LONELINESS

GEORGE ZANCOLA

I'm writing because the TED Talks didn't help,
and it's late, and there is no cable, and I'm tired.
And there is no window to the outside world,
and I'm thinking the starry scenes above must be
screaming like a silence, or some other
sheer mad poetry ripping within me.
And like bravado in solitude,
the voices persist in my monotone mania.
By scientific jargon, the confinement is given title
with a hell-bound twist on words like *darkness*,
and terms like *schizophrenic* are brokered
by inappropriate pronouns, and the poet in me
is the lover in me, and both entities are in disconnect.
No one could see me, and I could not shine in that light,
and I sought the improbable as wonder fractured
into many eyes, with no escape from the glare.

To the watchman I cried loud enough to be heard,
but he stared dead ahead into his own life.
He would allow no one access to my room,
except the nurse with a needle to stick in my arm.
She had memorized a manual of efficiency.
She was always on time.
I couldn't help but ask if hourly injections
would redeem me from an inability to see light.
And if they didn't work, she said,
there was shock treatment.

I remember again the dance of the watchman, and the nurse.
I recall the power moving through them, so hidden, obscene,
and they witnessed the power that moved in me.
I was frightened by the path they made into my solitude,
and they were frightened, too.

THE DESTINATION RHYME

GEORGE ZANCOLA

I'm inside the drop-
in for psychiatric
survivors, while one
who bled for
the world is telling me,
in a roundabout speech,
that she is short
twenty cents for a
twenty-five-cent
coffee sold
by the cup
at the counter near
the pool table

I'm so inside
the drop-in, the
police no longer
recognize me and real
women look upon
my existence harshly

I'm so inside
the drop-in
that it does not
seem too awful to deny
my partner twenty cents

I'm into this drop-in for
the redemption
hiding in corners,

in the tables and chairs, the
bloodied cull from the
laughingstock, the
sacrifice that cannot
be mouthed, the awk-
ward fear, the gold tooth
in your crown, the
gem from the fifth
bed in the row of twenty,
in the men's ward

I'm here, where the
radio hit still plays
in cruel repetition
through a haze of
obscurity, marking
passage from wild dan-
cing to medicated
civility

I'm in the drop-in,
being pushed,
while I ride
on the edges
of a fight

and weep
over the terms
given for surrender

THE RIBFEST PSYCHIC

HOWARD J. SANCHEZ

....

Rhianne and I decided to walk around the attractions at Ribfest. There were rides that looked unsafe along with sketchy-looking carnival games that seemed impossible to win. Big-name companies plugging their products so event-goers would either buy or sign up for their exclusive Ribfest promos. That one time-share seller who pretends they're not sus, even though no one believes them. Unless they were giving away minuscule free samples, the food vendors jacked up their prices like crazy. Large Toronto events like Ribfest have a tendency to cheese me every now and then. Luckily, I have a girlfriend like Rhianne who blessed me with his-and-her knock-off Raptors caps.

After checking out almost everything, she noticed a psychic within the pop-ups. Acting as a divider for the corporate pop-ups and the local ones. Rhianne was curious about it. I, on the other hand, was skeptical, especially in a place like this.

"Hun, we should get our palms read," said Rhianne.

"I don't know," I said. "It's not like what they say is true."

"But aren't you the least curious?"

"It's not like it's gonna make a difference."

I had a surprise in store for her later tonight, and getting our palms read might spoil it.

"C'mon, let's just check it out," said Rhianne. "Please?"

I whined as I finally gave in. "Fine, but don't be surprised if I say, *I told you so.*"

"Re-lax. You worry too much."

We approached the psychic's booth and went in. To be honest, I assumed the booth would be crowded by curtains, with an old Indian guy sitting across from us, idols placed on a table behind him, and the whole place smelling of incense. I couldn't have been further from the truth.

....

A white woman in her mid-twenties sat in front of a small table with a few crystals and some pamphlets. Two chairs were placed across from her, and a sign behind the table displayed the various psychic services she provided. The booth looked bland and boring, but at least there was no incense. If I did catch a whiff, I would've been outta there.

The psychic herself was friendly. She greeted us with a "Hey there" as we took our seats. "What can I do for you two?"

"Yeah, how much for a reading?" asked Rhianne.

"It's twenty dollars for one palm. For one of you."

Rhianne checked her wallet. "I only have enough for me."

"It's fine," I said. "I'll be here for moral support."

Rhianne pulled out twenty dollars and gave it to the psychic.

"Okay then, please stick out your dominant hand."

The psychic took a second to observe Rhianne's right hand. Slowly beginning to reveal what the future held for her.

"I see a good life for you. A life full of love, a life full of wealth, and a life full of happiness. So far, it seems like everything is perfect."

To my surprise, the psychic was accurate. I hadn't hired her, but she was making my job much easier.

"However…"

"What?" said Rhianne. "Is everything still okay?"

"I'm worried that all these blessings you currently have will be taken away from out of nowhere."

Yo, is this psychic for real? She can't just say something great, then follow it up with horrible news!

"What? You mean like death?"

"All I can say is that I advise you to treasure those closest to you. At any moment, everything will be taken away."

Enough was enough. I pulled Rhianne's hand from the psychic. I was fed up with the lies she was telling my girlfriend and, hopefully, soon-to-be fiancée.

"You know what, thank you for your time," I said. "If you'll please excuse us."

"But, Hunter—" said Rhianne, as I dragged her out of there. "The hell! Why'd you do that?"

"You don't expect me to believe those lies now, do you?" I asked.

"I wasn't serious, I was just curious," she said.

"Well, I guess that curiosity kills now, doesn't it," I said.

Rhianne punched me on my left arm, but it was definitely not a flirt punch.

"All right! I'm sorry! Geez!"

"Are you, Hunter, or are you just saying that to make me feel better?"

"C'mon now, you know I wouldn't let this 'psychic' hurt you."

"Well...she never hurt me to begin with."

A tear ran down her face. I realized I was in the doghouse as she started to walk away from me.

"Wait, Rhiannon. I'm sorry. I shouldn't have—"

"It's fine, but I don't want to talk to you right now. All this is too much, and I just...I just need a moment to myself."

"But—"

"I'll catch up with you in a bit, but just leave me alone for now. Can you at least do that?"

I watched her walk deeper into the safe-ish rides and carnival games. Once she was out of view, I headed toward the concession area to grab a much-needed cold one.

I made myself feel much worse than I needed to by coughing up five dollars for a cold glass of home-brewed, non-alcoholic, lemon iced tea. Drowning my misery by suffering in sobriety. Avoiding both light-headedness and the Asian flush as I tried to come up with a new plan for getting down on one knee.

After twenty minutes of taking minuscule sips of iced tea, I looked at my wallet. I was relieved that I hadn't spent all my money yet. With my last ten-dollar bill, I proceeded to the closest popcorn stand. At this rate, their eight-dollar lemon cotton candy was my last hope to ensure I could still pop the question.

Psyching myself up to go and apologize to Rhianne, I bought the cotton candy, only to realize she was waiting for me when I turned around. Carrying a plate of Blooming Onion fresh from the deep-fryer and a bowl of Maple Bacon Poutine on top. She wasn't as anxious as before, so giving her space had been the right choice. We took a moment to just stare at one another, until the wind blew the cotton candy onto my face.

"That was for me, wasn't it?" she asked.

Trying to salvage some dignity, I removed the cotton candy from my cheek. "Thought I'd cheer you up. Didn't you spend your last twenty already?"

"The poutine place accepts debit."

A few seconds of silence went by. My guilt from earlier came flooding back. "I still feel bad about before, and I can't apologize enough."

Rhianne rolled her eyes at me. "I know."

"I'm sorry I hurt your feelings," I said.

"Which you shouldn't have done in the first place."

"I'm still sorry, you know."

"I know you are!" A tear fell as Rhianne fought them back. "But you're not a bodyguard, you're my boyfriend. You don't have to protect me."

She walked right up to my side, leaning her head on my shoulder. I wrapped my arm around her waist. Then let out a big sigh. "Guess I was protecting myself."

"Ya think?" Rhianne said as she sniffled. "You may be a pain every now and then, but I don't know what I'd do without you."

I hugged her a little tighter as we headed for the exit.

"You'll still stay if what she said happens, right?" Rhianne asked quietly.

I turned my head toward her and gave her a kiss on the head. "Hey, as long as we're both alive, I don't need to rearrange the alphabet."

"I don't get it."

"Well, if you think about it, there's already a *u* in my name and—"

"You have better puns than that. You're Filipino."

There was a small line forming at the exit. I took a fry from Rhianne's poutine as we waited to leave.

"You know, it's just one psychic's opinion anyways," said Rhianne. "It's more credible if other psychics agree with her. Besides, she never gave us a specified time limit. It's not like my future's set in stone unless I set it myself."

"True. Like, any moment could just mean delivery complications or from natural causes when you're middle-aged. Those are probably bad exa—"

Rhianne silently inserted a Blooming Onion in my mouth. The deep-fried onion leaf was surprisingly juicy, yet bland.

"No Buttermilk Ranch Dip?" I asked while chewing.

"My poutine's on top of it."

"That's fine then." I went for a kiss on her cheek, only to kiss her right hand instead.

"Don't," said Rhianne. "You have onion breath."

"Sor-ry."

"Let's pretend the psychic fiasco never happened. Besides, I can feel my little sister spamming texts."

"Agreed. My li'l sis is doing the same."

"They should be setting up blankets at the diamonds with everyone else."

"Yeah, the fireworks start in a couple hours. Shall we?"

We left Ribfest and began our ten-minute walk toward the baseball diamonds. There was only an hour of sunlight left on this potentially epic Canada Day. I could already imagine how magical it was going to be to ask the question halfway through the fireworks. It was funny, though. Despite my determination, I'd never felt so nervous in my life.

"You good, Hun?" Rhianne asked.

I successfully smooched her cheek. "I'm always good when I'm with you, Rhianne."

MEMORIES OF DAWN

MARK HARVEY

....

I don't have much left
From our relationship
Except this one photograph
Of you and me together
Maybe you weren't drop-dead gorgeous
But you were prettier than you tended
To give yourself credit for
My skin was smoother back then
And I had more—and silkier—hair
Still, for the age I am now
My hair isn't bad

And I still have that greeting card you gave me
When I was going through rough times
The one that started with
"You haven't seemed yourself lately"
You died far too young
Still, I cherish and sometimes relive
Those moments that we had
And I think of you with a smile

BLUNTING THE EDGES OF NOSTALGIA

FATHUMA JAMA

I broke myself open
with a flighty, unmoored Sudani girl
over a sweet sticky summer
full of sin and possibility
frizzy twist-outs in buns
smelling faintly of vanilla and mango
paying no mind to tangled roots
giggling and exhaling into one another
in dingy shisha bars
when it felt like there was nowhere else
in this city to hide—from myself
with her, I almost forgot
to look over my shoulder

BLUEBERRY IMPRINTS

EUNICE CU

....

One. After three months of taking my basal body temperature at the ass-crack of dawn, it finally stays up. The temperature rise tells me that something has shifted in my body. It's a promising sign. A few days later, after an almost-blackout at the Sunday farmers' market, I lie down to recover in the back seat of my car. My brain makes comparisons to the time I had the flu when I was eight. Not some nasty head cold, but full-blown influenza. The feeling-faint-shiver-for-a-week-lying-in-a-puddle-of-your-own-sweat-and-projectile-vomiting-until-exhaustion-makes-eternal-sleep-seem-like-an-inviting-option kind of influenza. Then I remember the raised temperatures. Was I actually pregnant? Holy shit. What have I done?

Two. Yep. Pregnant. The stick is the first to tell me. Part of me is excited. Another part, shit-scared. Some other part is just freaking the hell out. I tell my husband. Years later, I will still be able to see his face; a faint smile, his nostrils lightly flaring, before promptly shutting down as he begins to drink his own cocktail of messed-up emotions.

Three. A positive blood test from my GP, and a week later we're at a nice restaurant celebrating the pregnancy and the end of my semester at uni. They have Bluff oysters on the menu and I can't resist, so we order half a dozen. Slippery, with a nice bite, they go down easy, leaving a salty sweetness and an aftertaste of metal and lemon in their wake. Oh, fuck. I wasn't supposed to have those. Nor those stolen sips of Riesling. Have I just killed this baby? Maybe it's for the best if I have. I clearly don't know what I'm doing. How the hell do I go without eating sushi for nine months? Shit. What else can't I eat? It begins to dawn on me how clueless and unprepared I really am.

....

Four. Amazon delivers *The Mayo Clinic Guide to Pregnancy* to my house a week later. I start reading. It has a whole section on pre-conception preparation and prenatal vitamins. This baby's only been brewing for a month, and already I feel like I'm behind on parenthood. Why didn't I think of reading this book *before* I got pregnant? I need to step up. I can't raise this kid the same clueless way my parents raised me. I won't. I need to do better. We *both* need to do better.

Five. My boobs hurt and they don't fit into the underwire bras anymore. I haven't gained weight exactly, but it feels like I have permanent period bloat and my clothes have shrunk in the dryer. I'm eating almonds like they're going extinct. I figure if I keep a constant flow in and down, it might dissuade my gut from hurling up and out. Plus, almonds are supposed to be good for the baby's brain, right? I walk uphill like an end-stage heart-failure patient, which might've been okay if this city didn't have So. Many. Fucking. Hills. I'm off my favourite foods. I've got the nose of a bloodhound. *And* I'm always tired. I'm not even showing yet, but I feel like an alien's taken over my body. This kid better be worth the damn trouble. You can bet I'll be telling them all about their fucking prenatal antics too.

Six. I'm struggling to stay awake long enough to concentrate on my university coursework. My doctor tells me I need to take it easy. Unenrolling-from-university level of easy. I'm in the middle of my post-grad. If I stop now, when am I going to finish it? My inner feminist rages. Why does this thing have to grow in *my* body? Why the hell is it *me* that needs to give up what *I'm* doing to incubate an alien for nine months? Why is it so damn hard to withdraw from university courses once you've enrolled? The world is unfair. Human biology is unfair. Fuck the world. Fuck bureaucracy. And fuck the institutions that support the patriarchy. I go home and ask my husband if he's read the baby book yet. I'm growing another *human*—*your* human—and you can't be bothered to read a damn book? Fuck men. Fuck you.

Seven. The book and the Internet tell me my baby alien is the size of a blueberry. We've nicknamed it ET. I think it's probably a girl but I'm not sure. I'm lying in bed with my head in the pit of my husband's arm. I tell him it's starting to feel like this is all on me. Isn't he scared we might screw up a human being if we don't get our act together? Does he think he's outgrown his childhood emotional neglect enough to avoid messing up our kid? Silence. His body tenses. Look, I get that he's always been on the quiet side and prone to acting childlike. But right now, that shit is making this *joint* and *very adult* undertaking seem extremely one-sided and lonely. Oh man, have I made a huge mistake? Who did I marry? What have I gotten myself into?

Eight. I sit in the driver's seat of my car. I've pulled over to a lookout to eat my Mediterranean eggplant sandwich. I look down at the straining elastic waistband of my blue skirt. I give it a pat. "Hey, kid, *I've* got you." I take a bite. My sandwich tastes good.

Nine. I'm at the radiology clinic. Today, I get to meet my alien. Cold ultrasound jelly. The sonographer makes some chit-chat. Asks me if I'm excited to finally get some photos of my baby. Then her face changes. "I'm having trouble picking up a heartbeat. I can see your bladder is full. The fluid might be obscuring the image. Could you try emptying it?" I'm sure it'll be fine. This'll all be okay. Baby, today's not the time to play hide-and-seek. I go back to the sonographer. She takes measurements and pictures. I ask her about the heartbeat. Her face communicates pity without her permission. I run out of the radiology clinic. Desperate. Foggy. Confused.

My mind dissects all the different ways this could go down. It ruminates. I'm booked in to see my GP later that day. I call my friend Martha and ask if she will wait out the hours with me. I'm worried about the places my imagination will wander if I'm left on my own. We go to the city wildlife sanctuary. I breathe in the dappled sunlight, rustling leaves, and evening birdsong. Then I look over at Martha. She looks like a possum in headlights. My messy feelings are junked in lieu of prattling on about the validity of old wives' tales. I'm now taking care of *her*. How did it come to this? I'm annoyed that the only people I've told about this pregnancy are like Martha—either single or don't have kids. Fucking clueless, the lot of them.

The GP tells me the fetus has died due to "incompatibility with life." Describing it here in this way makes him sound like a heartless fuck. He wasn't. He was actually really nice about it. I just wasn't in the mood to be consoled. He arranges an appointment at the hospital for a consult.

Another ultrasound. It's my luck that the doctor I get is extremely pregnant. The nurses at least ask me if I'm okay with that. I roll with it.

The doctor gives me some pills, and a little over a week, to see if the fetus will trigger a spontaneous abortion before they go in and surgically remove the "products of conception." My mind knows that my baby is dead, but my body still thinks it's alive—and the hormones it's pumping, they're messing with me. I decide to use this time to say goodbye.

"Stars" by Grace Potter & the Nocturnals plays. Your dad and I lie on our backs and look up at the Southern Cross through the sloping rear window of the station wagon. You and I have demolished our favourite burger and now he's showing you the constellations of the southern sky. We've been at it a few days now. Yesterday, I taught you about the different kinds of birds at the wildlife sanctuary, and the day before, the three

....

of us watched the planes try to stick gale-force landings at the airport. At home, we read you stories of Hairy Maclary and Badjelly the Witch. We want to leave you with as many childhood memories as we can.

I wake in the middle of the night to cramps in my belly. It feels like the kind of period pain that refuses to go until my uterus takes a crap—but much more intense. Much more than the mild analgesics can handle. Multiple rounds. A bathtub and a bucket. A sleepless night for all three of us. There is no ceremony in childbirth—not even for a blueberry-sized baby.

I'm grateful that my husband is at least there when we say goodbye. I don't think the marriage would've survived otherwise. But I'm bitter that he still hasn't read the damn book. Angry and betrayed when he says nothing while his mother tells me that getting pregnant again will help me feel less sad. Hurt, because it seems like he's moved on.

Melissa calls to ask how I am. She's heard about my miscarriage through Martha. I feel cheap. I listen to her recount all her friends' miscarriages in great detail and all the different ways they got through theirs. She reassures me that I will get through mine too. She asks me if it's okay to tell others close to us. I'm tempted to hurl my phone through a window. Better yet, I imagine smashing it on her face.

It turns out that *my community*, the one I had envisioned as my child-rearing village, aren't who I thought they were.

My community.

Some of these people I've known my whole life.

Not everyone is like this. Susan flies down and cooks my meals for a weekend to make sure I'm okay. Amy offers to take me out for coffee and share the story of her miscarriage. They are the exceptions—most of the support I find comes unexpectedly, from complete strangers. Women

....

who, during random tear-stained outbursts, offer a pat on the back or silent solidarity—a stark contrast to the sharp, intrusive counsel peddled by those presuming to know and care about me.

You helped me see the dumb shit that I was either too naive or too deep in denial to see. I haven't been able to look at many of these people in the same way. I clearly chose badly. Many of them I'm not even sure I want in my life anymore. You helped me realize how urgently I need a new community.

I bury you under a kōwhai tree in the children's section of the cemetery. When I fill in the forms for the burial, I have to call you a "placenta," otherwise the city council insists they will charge me the same amount for burying you as a fully grown adult. You didn't survive the first trimester; you are a nonentity to them.

Around that time, it occurs to me that, apart from a few medical letters, blood tests, and a patient wristband from my hospital admission, I have very little proof you ever existed.

And then I remember.

I get in my car.

I drive like a nutter and sprint into the radiology clinic. Sweaty. Breathless. Impatient.

For a picture of you.

Author's Note: Martha, Melissa, Susan, and Amy are composite characters who have been given pseudonyms. The author would like to thank Kathy Friedman and Sheniz Janmohamed for their mentoring and guidance in shaping this piece, as well as Maggie Brown and Barb Machina for their support while writing it.

A LIFE IN TEN

MG SHEPHERD

....

10. We met in Miss Hickey's Grade 1 class wearing cute dresses, because girls could not wear pants. My first vivid memory is of being at her house after school when her mother came home with new pillows.

9. She has severe hearing loss in one ear, a loss that occurred in childhood. But I could never recall which ear and usually walked on her wrong side.

8. She never had a chance to say goodbye to her mother—the day her father finally let her visit the hospital was the day Joan died.

7. She became a step-daughter eight months later. She found out her father was remarrying when a neighbour dropped by with congratulations. The wedding was small. She was not invited.

6. She has lived her life obsessed with dying of breast cancer.

5. She loved Dave more than he loved her.

4. When my father died, she was my rock, like a sister, unlike my real sister, and sat next to me in the church pew as I cried. A few days later we laughed when the minister confused her for my life partner, my love.

3. At eighteen she told me a man who truly knew and loved her would present her a sapphire—not diamond—engagement ring. When she was forty, he did.

2. She was a widow less than a year after marrying. Her father did not go north for the funeral.

1. Returning to her centre of the universe after several years in the cold north, she lives with loving cats in a house paid for by insurance. But a nice home does not replace love, belonging, and happiness.

....

WILSON AVENUE

DANA SAHADATH

I love the street I live on.
I bike, smoke, and spend my day walking it.
I adore all the people and say hello along the way;
I walk down Wilson Avenue
admiring the buildings, stores,
cars, and bikes passing by
on the sunny street;
I contemplate life in the Downsview Parkette
and take in the sounds of the cars gliding by and
the sight of windsocks blowing in the wind
to remind people that Downsview
was the manufacturing hub
for WWII aircraft—
the Gypsy and Tiger Moth.
I love Wilson Avenue
just as much
as Wilson Avenue
loves me.

BLOOD ORANGE

YASAMAN MANSOORI

....

I love blood oranges. I've loved them ever since I read *Black Ice*, Anne Stuart's miserable romance novel that I inexplicably found in my sixth-grade classroom and smuggled home to devour in private. My twelve-year-old self shook with desire for the steely, almost hateful Bastien as he hand-fed them in segments to Chloe before treating himself. "His mouth was close to hers. 'Tell me I'm a good man, Chloe,' he said in a soft, dead voice. 'Show me just how stupid you really are.'" Ah, romance.

"Blood oranges are the sexiest fruit," I said whenever the opportunity arose, scanning people's faces to see if they were as impressed with the sentence as I hoped. Invariably, they were absolutely not interested in discussing the erotic properties of citrus fruit, and I was greeted with flashes of discomfort as it occurred to my conversation partner that I likely had more to say on the subject. "No matter," I would think, "they're not sophisticated enough to understand." Onward I forged. For years I offered this observation to partners, secretly wishing that this time, finally, I would be met with enthusiasm. "Oh my God, yes. You are so right. They are rife with mystery and so tart they could slice your tongue. We must wed post-haste." To no avail.

Do I actually think blood oranges are sexy? Upon honest reflection, yes, I do. There's a suggestive sado-masochism about their exterior. Their skin punctuated with burgundy splotches—as if they were whipped the night before by a larger, more dominant counterpart. Perhaps a grapefruit. Fruit coitus aside, the sanguine gradients of mauve and maroon on a blood orange sliced sideways are undeniably beautiful. One can revel in the visual splendour of their existence.

Blood oranges are the troubled but more interesting sister of a regular navel orange. Navel oranges are so…consistent. So yes, you're an orange. Peel, peel. Very good. Thanks for the vitamin C.

It is on the backs of navel oranges that the hoi polloi of society were able to curb scurvy. It is the navel orange that feeds children, fills grocery

....

stores, and wards off illness. They serve an indispensable function. The blood orange excites me. It is the blood orange I want to ask every question. What were you like as a child? Where were your sanctuaries? Do you remember the sound of your own laughter? Whose was the first hand you held that wasn't a grown-up? What lies did you tell for so long they became truths?

Blood oranges aren't everyone's favourite. They have a thicker, tougher skin (are we surprised?). Their tartness borders on the acidic, and even tastes bitter to some. There is an impracticality to the blood orange that makes them more of a treat than a staple. But they like that just fine. Blood oranges never set out to be everyone's favourite. Blood oranges' depth of colour betrays their rich inner life. Inscrutable. A kaleidoscope of personality. Their stains more stubborn. Their possession a secret bliss against the backdrop of the ordinary.

Show me a blood orange and I'll show you my guts.

ENJOY YOUR MORNING BREW, NICE AND SLOW!

ASPI KOOTAR

Some pals stay, while others go
Enjoy your brewed Tim Hortons, nice and slow

Breathe slowly when your kids choose to go
In which country, you don't care to know

America, Canada, or Australia, it don't matter
Enjoy your brewed Tim Hortons, NICE AND SLOW!

SKELETON COASTER

ASUKA LAPIERRE

....

Everyone around me is getting worse
bit by bit, losing their will to live
and I'm the only one pushing them forward.
No one can know
that I am what holds them together
or the whole system fails.
No one thinks of my
old, rusty, unreliable body

when they're running on adrenaline.
Clack, clack, clack.
I possess the potential energy
but they're constantly weighed down—
I have to keep adding force
when I have so little left.
Kinetic energy takes over
and before I know it
they're hurtling toward a desolate land.
I only push them forward
for them to crash down again,
and again, and again.
The rush of falling
has become addictive.

DESPONDENT

MICHELE BRETON

....

I
of
our
fine
ocean
feared
quickly
becoming
poisonous
despondent

FRAGMENTS

ADAM ZABOROWSKI

....

First line by Tomaž Šalamun

Fragments, only fragments
A shattered mind like broken glass
cuts the hands of those who care
They want to help, want to share
but they feel only fragments
fragments everywhere.

THE TASTE OF HOME

NORIKO HOSHINO

When I turned six, I was told that my birth parents lived elsewhere. I was confused. Weren't Mother and Father real? They didn't want me anymore? Had I been a bad boy? After my initial shock wore off, I became curious about the other family and tried to imagine my life there, but I couldn't picture myself in a town I'd never seen. The only world I knew was a small farm in a hamlet called Old Pond.

It was the second Saturday in November, after harvest, when my foster father, Ryoji, took me to town. We got up at dawn to catch a train. He wheeled a handcart to the station in the village. He grunted as he lifted a tall frame pack off the cart and slung it onto his back. Large baskets full of vegetables were stacked up high and secured to the frame.

On the platform I heard the whistle in the distance. The gigantic caterpillar with iron armour belched white steam that streamed above its russet body and beyond. The rhythmic chug was getting closer and the train rumbled into the station. Ryoji swung the door open. I darted in and jumped onto the seat.

Hissing, the train lurched forward. The platform pillars started to slide. The power poles flew by. The mulberry field was a misty blur with shadowy mountains behind it.

Soon the train trundled into the next station. The hum went dead. When the conductor said something, Ryoji opened his eyes and yawned. But soon his eyelids drooped and his head hung over his crossed arms. I looked around. Frame packs were set on the waxed floor in front of the men with tanned, leathery faces. Nothing outside the window moved. My birth parents would be waiting for me. They knew I was coming home.

I pulled Ryoji's sleeve. "Why aren't we moving?"

He strained to lift his eyelids. "Because we have to wait for the freight train."

"Why?"

"Because," he said with a sigh, "this is a single-track railway, so we have to let it pass."

"Can't we go first?"

"Can't. Do you know why Mount Buko is white?"

"No."

"It's made of limestone. They built the railroad to haul limestone. They don't care about human cargo."

"Who are 'they'?"

"Rich people."

Arriving in town, we went to the grocery store. Ryoji unloaded most of the vegetables in the baskets. Then we visited a couple of relatives, having tea at the first and lunch at the second. When we finally reached my birth parents' place, it was already mid-afternoon.

After lengthy greetings, some gifts changed hands: produce from Ryoji and an ornate mirror from my mother. All the while I was looking down at the toes of my canvas shoes.

"I'll come back later to pick up Mutsu," said Ryoji.

"Will you let him stay overnight?" Mother asked. "I'll have his brothers walk him back to Old Pond tomorrow."

I wasn't sure if I wanted to stay overnight. I certainly did not want to miss the train ride back. But I didn't speak. A good boy would not interrupt adult conversations. Ryoji agreed. Another round of greetings followed. He left to visit yet another relative.

Mother knelt down and held my face gently with her coarse but warm hands. "Oh, my Little Moo, you've grown!"

I didn't have any memory of her dark brown eyes or raven-black hair, but her voice rocked my heart. Her eyes lingered on me for another moment.

"Come," she said, and led me to the back of the house, where she had been shelling soybeans.

Tan beans were spread on a large sheet of brown paper in the engawa corridor that overlooked the garden. The rest of the engawa was covered with futons, soaking up the sun.

"It's your baby brother, Shichi." Mother pointed at a young boy napping on the futon.

"Shichi, like 'seven'?"

"Yes, he's the seventh child."

I thought about my name. It meant "harmony" but it was pronounced the same as "six," which always made me feel less important. But my brother got an actual number.

I sat beside Mother. She broke the tip, split the shell, and popped the beans out. Her hands moved swiftly and steadily. Rhythmic snaps punctuated the silence.

Her hands still moving, she looked up. "Do they treat you well?"

"Yes, Mother."

"Are you being a good boy all the time, Little Moo?"

"Yes, Mother. Almost always."

"Almost?"

"I mean, always."

"Good."

We fell silent again. I glanced at an ancient persimmon tree in the garden. The plump flaming-orange fruits clustered along the branches added the final shine to the late-afternoon sky.

"Ah, persimmons," said Mother, noting the objects of my interest. "They aren't the sweet kind. Even when ripe, they have such a biting taste that you can't even swallow them."

"I thought all persimmons were sweet."

"No. But there are ways to make them sweet."

"How?"

"By drying them in the sun, for one. The bitterness will turn into a sugary, rich taste. We could soak them in shochu too, but your father would rather keep all sake and shochu to himself."

"Sunshine is free."

"Right. It's for everybody, rich or poor." She smiled for the first time. "I've already started hanging persimmons. See, up there?"

My eyes followed her index finger. Dozens of shrivelled lumps hung on the threads from the bamboo pole under the eaves. Their dark surfaces had tiny white dots resembling mildew.

"They taste a lot better than they look," said Mother.

I wondered how she knew what I was thinking.

"When you go back tomorrow, take some with you. They should be ready by now."

Hearing the words "go back," my heart sank.

"Don't worry. Your brother will carry them for you."

This time she misread my thought. She wasn't a sorceress after all.

"Do you want vegetable tempura for dinner? Ryoji-san brought us some vegetables. Cooking oil is expensive these days, but this is a special occasion."

"I like tempura."

"I'd better get started. They say the autumn sun sinks as quickly as a bucket falling into the well. Your brothers and sisters are coming back shortly, except for the oldest one, Masaru. He's off to college." She gathered the beans and put them into a bamboo basket. "Little Moo, wake up your baby brother and keep an eye on him, will you?"

Soon my siblings returned, one after another. Every time someone came home, I was reintroduced to them. I felt awkward and sensed that the feeling was mutual. My baby brother was the only one who showed no reservations, following me everywhere.

....

When the dinner was ready, Father sat on his floor cushion at the head of the long, low table. His skin was dark. Unlike Ryoji's tanned, healthy-looking complexion, Father's face was an earthy colour. His eyes, under bushy eyebrows, held my gaze. The whites took up a lot of his eyes, and only the upper halves of the dark brown irises were visible. I felt pinned to the wall.

A family dinner of eight was not something I was accustomed to; I was the only child at my farmhouse. It was odd, though—this gathering was much quieter than I had expected. The only sound was the clicking of chopsticks touching rice bowls. Everything was done in such an orderly manner that we could have been at the Emperor's banquet. Even my baby brother sat properly, his back erect and his legs folded neatly under him.

Father broke the silence. "Mutsu, you seem healthy. Health is important. You cannot accomplish anything if you are weak."

"Yes, Father," I replied, straightening my back.

"Ryoji-san and Shizu-san seem to be taking good care of him," said Mother.

"Mutsu is a lucky boy. He will never know hunger. After all, they are farmers."

Mother nodded in agreement.

Then the others started to talk about their day. I looked around the table so I would remember everyone's face till I came home next, although I did not know when that would be.

I woke up at daybreak. It felt strange to find myself among my brothers, who were still sound asleep on the futons placed side by side in the six-tatami room. I lay in semidarkness, listening to the peaceful breathing of my brothers interrupted by occasional snores.

....

Breakfast was less formal than dinner the night before, but nearly as quiet. After we finished, Mother made some rice balls. She put a pickled plum in the centre of each and toasted them on a grill over the hibachi while spreading soy sauce on their surfaces with a brush. Then she wrapped them in bamboo sheaths, put them in a brown paper bag, and placed them in a sack, on top of the small cardboard box full of dried persimmons.

Father said to his second son, "Kashio, walk Mutsu back to Old Pond. You can take Yo along so you'll have company on your way back."

When we were about to leave, Mother draped her arms around me. She smelled of charcoal mixed with the aroma of singed rice and soy sauce.

While we marched along the dirt lane, I looked back at the house over and over again. Every time I turned around, Mother waved her hand. We turned onto the main street, but I knew she was still there.

When I'd arrived the day before, I'd been so preoccupied with my first visit to my birth family that I hadn't paid much attention to the surroundings. Now that I was about to leave the place, I felt an urge to take in every detail. The general store still had straw hats and rubber thong sandals near the front. The school, the town hall, the community centre, and a police booth clustered near the station.

"Li'l Moo, your head turns like an owl," said Yo. "Do you see your own tail feathers?"

"I don't have a tail."

"He's just teasing you," said Kashio. "There's nothing much to see here, though. Some people call it Pee Brook Township."

"Why?"

"They say it looks like a tiny flow of trickling piss. It's got hardly any space to spread out because of the mountains sitting on both sides."

We walked past the last house in town and came to a bend. The road veered to the northeast and disappeared behind the brow of a hill.

Kashio stepped onto a narrow footpath that tapered off down the pebbled slope. "This is a shortcut. The trains don't come very often, so we should be all right."

On the left side of the track, along the slope, stood evening primroses—withered flowers on top of the bone-dry stalks with brown strips that used to be leaves. On the right, towering pampas grasses rippled in the wind. We walked single file, Kashio leading the way and Yo keeping guard at the end when he wasn't teasing me. We had a short break twice and, sitting on large stones by the river, ate lunch at a clearing when the sun was high up.

"We should have brought the fishing rods," said Kashio.

"Yeah. Why didn't we think of that?" Yo chimed in. "Rice balls are boring."

"But I like these rice balls," I said.

"Oh, come on, Li'l Moo. Don't tell me you've never eaten rice balls."

"I have, but not the toasted ones."

"You're kidding! We eat them all the time."

"I wish I could," I said, more to myself.

Kashio leaned over to pick up a flat round pebble and threw it sideways toward the river. The pebble skipped on the water's surface. "Four," he said.

Yo threw his pebble. "Damn! Only three."

"Here, try this," said Kashio, handing me a small flat stone. "Aim low, close to the surface."

I threw. "Only one."

"Not bad for a first-timer," said Kashio.

I tried a few more times, and now the stone skipped twice.

"You're getting better, Little Moo."

"How old are you?" I asked Kashio.

"Fourteen. Why?"

. . . .

"Just wondering."

"*I'm* ten," said Yo. "How old are *you*, Li'l Moo?"

"Six."

"Ha! Number Six is six now! Your name is 'six,' right?"

"It means 'harmony.'"

"But it sounds like 'six'," said Yo. "Mine is just like that. I don't like the sound of it because it's the same as 'four.' But 'Yo' means ocean. I'll do a big thing when I grow up."

"There's no number in your name," I said to Kashio.

"Mine's worse. 'Kashi' means woodmouse, the year I was born in. Big Brother is the only one who's got a decent name. Masaru means 'the superior one.' Our father's expectations are hard to miss. I hate to say it, but the rest of us are insurance policies."

"Li'l Moo, do you know our father works for an insurance company?"

"What's that?"

"Never mind," said Yo.

"When your house catches fire and you lose everything, they give you money so you can buy clothes and furniture. That's how insurance works," said Kashio. "We're the backup."

We got back on the train track again. I was getting tired and soon started to lag behind. We took breaks more frequently. Finally we came to a bridge, which led to the village. While we were still on the bridge, we heard a faint rumble.

"Run!" shouted Kashio.

We made a mad dash. Yo flew past me. Seconds later the bridge started to vibrate. I looked back and saw a steam locomotive coming out through the walls of dead primroses and pampas grass. The whistle shrieked.

"Jump off the bridge!" yelled Kashio.

He vanished. Yo followed. They landed on the riverbank. I crouched, swung my feet off the bridge, and lowered my body. But I held on to the edge of the railroad tie. My brothers shouted at me, telling me to let go, but my fingers were glued to the wood. The bridge started to shake. The metal wheels screeched. My mouth froze in the shape of a scream. Whirling air peppered dust into it.

The train finally gone, I suddenly felt numb. I fell. My brothers caught me and we tumbled to the ground. I wasn't hurt but I cried. The terror broke the dam that held all the tears I hadn't shed—when I learned that I'd been given away like a puppy, when I'd thought my Old Pond parents hadn't wanted me, and when I'd parted with Mother that morning. My brothers took my hands and we climbed back onto the tracks. We trekked in silence.

By the time we came to the edge of the village, I was so tired I couldn't walk any longer. Kashio gave me a piggyback ride while Yo carried the sack of dried persimmons. Kashio was thin but tall, and the ears of pampas grasses were now at my eye level. The village looked different.

"Why can't I stay with my own family?"

"Well, Little Moo—"

"Why me?"

"I don't know," mumbled Kashio. "But it could have been any one of us."

"It's not that I don't like my Old Pond parents. I thought they were my real parents. It's just…I like Mother."

"You can visit us again."

"I don't know if I'm allowed to. Besides, you'll forget about me soon."

"I won't. None of us will."

I rested my cheek on his shoulder.

At my farmhouse, my Old Pond mother, Shizu, prepared us an early dinner. My brothers shovelled food into their mouths as if they had not eaten for days. I was more tired than hungry, but I ate anyway.

After the late-afternoon meal, my brothers left for home. The living room suddenly became empty. I stared at Shizu, trying to search for features that were similar to Mother's.

"Mutsu, why are you looking at me like that?"

"I'm wondering if you and my birth mother look alike."

"She and I are second cousins. When we were kids, some people said we looked like sisters. But I haven't seen her for a while. What do *you* think?"

"I don't know," I said. But I knew. Shizu's eyes were animated and the corners of her mouth went slightly up as if she was always smiling. Mother didn't have that sunny streak. Maybe Shizu had been eating sweet persimmons all her life. I realized I hadn't studied her features this closely for a long time. Her face had become a little round and her cheeks rosy. Her body looked slightly plumper than before.

Later that evening when I was alone in my room, I opened the cardboard box. I picked up a dried persimmon and took a bite. The softened tissues released a sweet, rich flavour in my mouth. Mother. I savoured the memory of the warm afternoon with her.

When I woke up the next morning, I still felt weary. I looked around, unconsciously searching for my brothers. My futon looked small in the spacious room. I got dressed and went outside. After I washed my face and drank cold water from the well, I walked to the outhouse. I cried in the dark toilet, bidding farewell to the food I'd eaten, the food Mother had cooked for me.

THE RED BLANKET

JAMES WAGSTAFF

Colt, a teenage boy in foster care, was walking down the street when he tripped, falling and bumping his head. He lay unconscious for what seemed like hours. When he woke up, he was wrapped in a musty red blanket.

Colt figured someone must have thought he was homeless and covered him with it. The blanket was faded and worn, so he chucked it into a garbage bin. But as he turned to walk on, the blanket suddenly appeared on the ground in front of him.

"How did that happen?" he wondered, as the blanket slid between his feet and tripped him.

However, before he landed on the ground, the blanket lifted into the air and caught him.

"What the heck? A flying blanket," Colt said.

"What can I do for you?" the blanket asked.

"You speak—I must be dreaming!" the boy exclaimed.

"No, you aren't dreaming. My name is Lincon, and I am yours to command."

"You have a name?" Colt asked.

"Of course I do! You sound surprised."

"Well, it's not every day that I meet a talking blanket. Okay, Lincon, my name is Colt."

"Where would you like to travel to? I can bring you anywhere," Lincon proclaimed.

"I've always wanted to travel to England," Colt said.

"To England we go then."

The blanket scooped Colt off his feet and soon they were flying. The higher the blanket went, the more scared Colt became. But after a while he got used to it.

Lincon flew fast. Together they passed many trees, cornfields, and buildings. They flew across the ocean in record time. The blanket was slower than a plane but much more fun. It never faltered because it was the only thing between Colt and the ocean.

When they reached England, Lincon suggested that Colt pack him in a duffle bag, so as not to arouse suspicion.

They passed some of the nation's most beautiful farmlands and castles. Colt saw the Big Ben clock tower and heard it ring loudly when it struck the hour. He also saw Stonehenge, the great ruins themselves, and Buckingham Palace, where the royals live.

Colt didn't have any money for food, so he persuaded a restaurant owner to hire him as a dishwasher in exchange for meals. The owner agreed and fed him delicious pork chops, soda pop, string beans, and mashed potatoes. After two weeks of washing dishes and touring the sights, Colt was ready to head home.

"You will fly me back to Canada, won't you?" he asked the blanket.

"Yes, but there is something you should know," Lincon said.

"I knew it—it's always too good to be true."

"It isn't that bad really," Lincon said.

Colt sighed a second time. "Okay, spill it.

"For every hour of flight, you will age one day. You see, I am a magical blanket. I've lived for over five hundred years. I have had many owners. As of this moment, I have taken twenty days out of your life. If you use me too much, you will grow old extremely quickly. You may even die if you travel on me too much."

"Can I stop whenever I want?"

"Yes, but it's not that easy—flight becomes an addiction. It's hard to stop at that point. I advise you not to use me for more than three or four months. After that it will be too late to turn back."

"Okay, I will keep that in mind," Colt said. "Can we go to Egypt next?"

"Are you sure? That destination will take sixty days out of your life. Is that a price you're willing to pay?" asked Lincon.

"Yeah," Colt replied eagerly, "I want to see the pyramids."

"As you wish, climb on."

Colt did so, and in no time they were headed to Egypt. Once they landed, Colt put the red blanket in a duffle bag again. While he was there, he actually rode on a camel. He also saw the pyramids and the tombs of the pharaohs, including King Tut's famous resting place. When he went inside a pyramid, he noticed the air was stale and made a whistling sound. Colt felt hieroglyphics on the wall with his hand. It was a spooky and thrilling experience, and he didn't want the feeling to stop.

Colt was in Egypt for a week before he asked Lincon to take him to Australia.

"Are you sure you want to do that, Colt? It will be cutting it a little close," Lincon said.

"Yes, I want to see koalas and kangaroos."

Lincon did as Colt told him. It was not his place to argue the matter.

Colt saw kangaroos jump in the wild, and a koala climbing a tree and feeding on eucalyptus leaves. It was like something out of a storybook.

While he was in Australia, he met some locals who showed him their village. The men offered Colt stew, cheese, tea, and a place to stay. The stew not only smelled good, but it tasted good as well. Once he'd finished his meal, they told Colt some scary ghost stories that made him jump out of his shorts.

Eventually, he had had his fill of the sights, and he ordered Lincon to take him back home.

By the time Colt reached Canada, he had spent four months of travel on the magical blanket, and he still wanted to travel more. Lincon had warned him what would happen, but Colt didn't listen. He felt invincible.

Colt now wanted to travel to every country, even though it meant he could lose his life. He ordered Lincon to travel the world with him, and Lincon had to obey.

After two years of travelling, Colt was an old man. No one would miss him. His legal guardians cared only about the money they were getting for fostering him. He was travelling the world! How many people could say that? Although Colt now looked like a man in his late seventies, he was actually no older than seventeen. The addiction he'd been warned about didn't matter to him at this point, even though he was getting so old he could barely move. His bones were becoming aged and brittle.

And then Colt died.

However, it didn't stop there. What Lincon had failed to mention was what would happen after he died on the blanket.

The flying blanket turned his body to ashes and consumed his soul. This was why the blanket had lived for hundreds of years. The purpose of the magical blanket's existence was to consume energy in its rawest form and prey on the unwanted, for the unwanted were easy targets.

Lincon, now Colt, was an evil presence that fed on others' greed, and in this case the greed was an addiction to travel.

HOW TO MAKE A STIR-FRY

PAMELA CHYNN

....

Take a wok out. Oh no, you forgot, you burned that one the last time you were driven to make a stir-fry. That's okay. Your cast-iron pan will do. Take out those veggies—those organic substitute voodoo dolls. Oh yes, don't forget carrots. Exfoliate those dirty bastards with your cheese grater. Scrape. Scrape. Scrape. Next: the celery. Amputate the leaves but don't throw them away. Seal them in a ziplock bag. Tuck them into a dark corner of your freezer. Like memories, freeze them, in case someday you need them again. Just don't forget them like you did with all those vegetable peelings you kept, intending to make broth. After two years, the newspaper recipe you taped to your fridge has started to yellow. Just like some of the other recipes, which look like autumn leaves on the side of your fridge. Oh, get over yourself! Your poetic bullshit is what got you into this mess in the first place! Isn't that your MSG—your poetry? Verses have become your potato chips. It's not an autumn yellow but a pissy yellow—that's right, get real, bitch, get with the program. The colour of piss always makes you think of Jackson Pollock—his anger at Peggy Guggenheim's party of pretentious posers. He got so fed up, he pissed in the fireplace and the bourgeoisie went into convulsions of shock. Only time you ever experienced penis envy, when you learned of that one. Maybe you're just romanticizing the rebel in Pollock. Perhaps he just had too much to drink and made an ass of himself. But those vegetables, you had to throw them out—skins of onions, beets, potatoes, zucchini, and squash, evidence of your poor planning when you realized they were incubating in thick shells of frost, nesting in the back of the fridge, like baby chicks waiting to be hatched. Baby chicks are cute, but eggs taste so good on Sunday mornings drizzled with hot sauce. Screw it. Life's too short to make everything from scratch. Prepackaged dreams make life simpler. Besides, skin, like memories, contains as many toxins as nutrients, so it's just as well those peels end up in the garbage instead of in soup. Peel those potatoes. Don't take too much of the flesh with the

....

skin, as you are prone to do, being a southpaw. And now your favourite part. *Tell me something, are you feeling lucky, punk? Make my day.* Chop. Chop. Chop. No more Ms. Nice Guy. Chop. Chop. Chop.

THE MANGO

PAMELA CHYNN

....

When I dream of you,
I am
a mango
cradled in the shadow of the trees
bathing in its coolness

You are
the sun
shifting
through the branches
seeping
into my pores

until

I

blush sunsets
in places
where
you
have touched

me

ABSTRACTIONS

HONEY NOVICK

In the pursuit of happiness
I trained like an Olympic athlete
disciplined toward the expectation
of seeing my self-image in new ways.

Truth appears only to those
willing to see the invisible. They are gifted
with vision. Truth is the elephant in the room
taking up space, sucking up air
craving attention, drawing taunts.

Resilience stands up to the Dragon of Despair
as it hovers above like a buzzing gnat
determined to quash my aspirations
till I'm ready to confront this enemy
and stare at it until it melts.

Brilliance is the clothing I wear
to gingerly open the door of my vulnerabilities
those imperfections and sensitivities
as I point to the love I seek to protect.

Anger is the ocean I plunge into after touching your heart
having found the key to unlock the ocean's secret:
hidden, roiling, boiling, seething, churning.
I could dive in, but I froze knowing
that once I did, the ocean's rage would calm.
Still I couldn't move.

Abstractions (continued)

....

Night is always there—taunting:
"You don't know what I keep, what I give."
"No," I reply, "I don't."
This is not a mystery.
This is a lesson taught to seekers of knowledge.

"Give me courage," I say.
"Let me never diminish another.
This is what I want.
Night, if you cannot give me this
do not fear—
I am stronger than you and
will *not* diminish your power."

WHAT ALL THE RAGE IS

LORETTA FISHER

Doing only what's decent can lead to decent work—
not favouring profits over people, as if money counts first
Working class barely scraping by but always overworked
No overtime pay and paid mere crumbs off the pie
which is owned by one big corporate executive guy
who enriches himself by paying his workers peanuts (no lie)
and ignores your safety so you get injured—or die
These tragedies happen to workers all the time
and companies never get sued or even fined!
Recovering from injury but somehow deemed perfectly fine
accused of relying on rich taxpayers' charitable graces
Are wicked welfare queens and queue-jumpers *really* off to the races?
We're supposed to be eligible for benefits, but bosses lie to our faces
Workers are taxpayers too. Good grief!
So who is the *real* thief?
Our dignity is stolen under the guise of relief.

More of us rage against racial, economic, and ecological oppression!
But dividing the working class further erodes the foundation
of this stolen nation
The working class is the hands and feet supporting the congregate
but the 1% will bite off their own nose to spite their face
they can't see how stepping on us affects their own fate!
How long will we survive this racism *and* lack of paid sick days?
Shouldn't we bring our petitions for fairness to elected officials?
Asking for decency for people and the earth
should not lead to dismissals and court injunctions
RCMP raids, arrests over Indigenous rights
What's next: missiles?
Unless they recognize that our connection is truth

....

We're all equal members of humanity
from the basement up to the roof
Ontarians fighting for $15 and fairness is proof
Canadians marching beside Indigenous youth
We fight for decent work, fair wages, and green job positions
no more earth-polluting pipelines—a clean and just transition!
Can you hear our chants echo worldwide for real systemic changes?
This I believe is what all the rage is.

ZAYA

KOSHALA NALLANAYAGAM

....

Zaya was eight years old and the colour of chocolate. Her hair was blue-black and curly and her eyes were big and brown. She had a faraway look in her eyes. She was present in body but her mind and soul were somewhere else. But she was always ready with a big smile when anybody did get her attention.

Zaya wanted to be helpful to her parents but she was always breaking or spilling something or running into some object, so her mother asked her to stay away from the projects she was working on. Although Zaya understood the reason, it still made her sad.

Her dad would ask if she would like to polish his shoes and she was thrilled. Gathering the polish, brush, rags, and shoes, off she'd go to one of her favourite spots: the window seat in her bedroom that overlooked the garden. She was very proud of her accomplishment, especially when her dad complimented her on it.

Watching movies and TV shows like *Fame* sparked a fascination with dancing in Zaya. Standing in front of her bedroom mirror, she would try to copy the dancers' moves. Although Zaya hadn't shared her love of dance with her family or friends, she hoped that one day she could dance for everyone.

It was a challenge for Zaya to focus on the subject at hand at school. Although she was often in her dream world or distracted, she was well-liked by most of her classmates because she was kind, helpful, and funny. However, some of the others liked to laugh at her expense. These bullies teased her because she was so dreamy and absent-minded and they thought she behaved oddly. Poor Zaya! She would cry and then be laughed at even more.

Recess was her favourite subject. She didn't have trouble focusing on eating and playing and talking to her friends.

One Friday morning, Zaya walked in the door of her home with a smile on her face and called out, "Hi, Mom, I'm home!"

....

"What are you doing here, sweetie—are you all right?" her mother asked.

"Of course, Mom, I'm home for lunch!"

"But Zaya, it's only ten o'clock!"

"What! I...I...thought it was lunchtime. It felt like it should be. Why do I always do these stupid things? What am I going to do now!" Zaya started to cry.

"It's okay, sweetie, I'll take you back to school and explain it to your teacher. It'll be all right."

Zaya was inconsolable and told her mother she did not want to go back to school. However, her mother insisted that she return. Zaya was still crying when her mother took her back to class. Her mom and teacher stepped into the hall outside the classroom to talk, and Zaya walked slowly to her desk with her head down. She sensed everybody's eyes on her and did not want to return anyone's gaze. The teacher soon came back in and the class continued. But Zaya knew this was not going to be the end of it and she dreaded the consequences.

After school the bullies were waiting for her. They asked loudly, "Zaya, how come you don't know the difference between recess and lunch? Are you a spacey baby? Do you know what time it is now?" They screeched with laughter, and Zaya just wanted to shrink into the earth and disappear. She tried hard not to cry, but the tears flowed anyway. "Crybaby, crybaby..." they chanted, and she ran as fast as she could away from them. Even when she was out of earshot, she felt like she could still hear them.

Her parents didn't know about this or any of the other times she got teased. Zaya did not inform her parents because she knew it would make them sad and she also did not want them talking to her teachers or the principal, which would only make things worse.

One day there was an announcement at school about auditions to be a part of a dance crew that would perform at the upcoming fundraiser for parents and the community. Zaya perked up as soon as she heard "dance" and concentrated on listening to the full announcement.

She was very excited to tell her parents. "Mom, Dad, I am going to audition for a dance thing at school! Isn't that cool?"

Her mom and dad looked surprised.

"Well, dear, that's quite amazing," her mom said.

"It sounds like fun, Zaya," said her dad.

Later, her parents talked among themselves. "It's great that she is taking an interest in something at school, but *dancing?*" said her dad. "She can barely walk without running into something or tripping! I hope she's not setting herself up for a fall, literally!"

"Let's see how it goes," replied her mom. "You never know..."

The five judges at the audition were made up of teachers and senior students. The dancers had to learn a short jazz routine taught to them by the gym teacher, who was also a dance coach. All the participants had to demonstrate that they knew the steps but they also had to keep the pace with the others. Surprisingly, Zaya was able to do this rather well. She seemed like a natural and was chosen to be one of the dancers. She was looking forward to practising her dance routine!

Mom and Dad had been told that she wanted them to wait until the concert to see her dance. She spent many hours practising at school and at home in her room behind closed doors.

Finally, the big day arrived. The gym where the fundraiser was taking place looked good and didn't smell bad! It almost looked like a real auditorium. There was an atmosphere of excitement. Zaya was glad she was feeling good and not nervous. It was a great relief to her that she could wear tights and a shirt instead of a dress. Dresses made her feel uncomfortable and like she just couldn't be herself.

There was a lot going on around her. Other performers ran around wearing a variety of costumes. Some had dressed like animals, while others wore fancy shimmery dresses, magician's hats, and many other outfits appropriate for their particular performance. There were going to be magic shows, comedic skits, singing, and, of course, dancing. Since Zaya didn't have to do too much to get ready for the performance, she peeked from behind the curtains on the stage to check out the audience, especially her parents. She was glad to see her mom and dad sitting close to the front.

Zaya's parents were waiting in excited but nervous anticipation. When it was finally time for the dance number, they were overjoyed to see their klutzy daughter dancing well and looking like she was on top of the world!

But when Zaya looked out into the audience and saw her parents' faces, she stumbled and fell. The bullies started laughing. However, she managed to quickly get back in step with the other dancers and finished the rest of the performance perfectly. At the end, her parents were on their feet, cheering. Zaya beamed with pleasure and pride when she took her bow.

INVASIVE SPECIES

DONNA COOKE

....

Craig staggered into his building from his last gruelling night shift, his head throbbing. He had "agreed" to give up ten hours a week during the pandemic to help keep the struggling factory afloat. Yet here he was two weeks later—no severance pay from the job he'd held for three years. Fifteen minutes earlier, St. Mark's Hospital had phoned him so he could talk briefly with his elderly mother, who had COVID. She sounded scared, confused. They both were. Craig shivered at the thought that it might be the last time he would ever talk to her. He absent-mindedly opened his door, when a dog jumped up and started barking. *Wrong apartment!* He quickly pulled the door shut and turned across the hall, fumbling for his keys.

The old Union Avenue apartment had been Craig's home for over five years. Everything had been going well until four months ago, when Kim moved in across the hall with his stupid beagle. Bao's constant barking kept Craig up in the afternoons when he was trying to sleep. Complaining to the super didn't help. He was the only tenant home on their floor during the day, and the super said no one else had a problem. Craig brought up the noise with Kim once when they ran into each other on the elevator.

"Nonsense!" Kim had replied. "Bao's a quiet, well-behaved boy and he rarely barks."

Craig could barely control the urge to punch Kim. "Why don't you go back where you came from? You don't belong here!" he'd snapped.

Kim had turned red and rushed out of the elevator, swearing. Realizing he would have to solve his problem some other way, Craig started fantasizing about options, things he'd seen in movies…

Now Craig had the rare opportunity he'd been hoping for. Revenge. *It's because of these Chinese that my life's been turned upside down,* he thought. *How dare they spread COVID!* Killing Bao himself seemed appalling. Besides, he would be the prime suspect and everyone would blame him.

....

A mysterious disappearance would be better. He needed to act fast. In his fridge sat some leftover roast beef. Craig carved out a three-inch chunk and poured Benadryl all over it. He sniffed the meat, but it didn't smell any different. Craig opened the unlocked door to Kim's place and tossed the meat quickly onto the vinyl kitchen floor off the entryway. Bao growled menacingly but didn't bark as Craig slammed the door.

Back in his own place, Craig paced back and forth. *Was the world coming to an end?* He was sure his was. Craig looked out his fourth-floor balcony and wondered if jumping would be fatal. A loud grumbling from his gut startled him into remembering he hadn't eaten in over eight hours. But there was no hunger—only nausea and loneliness. He tried to eat some bread, but it stuck in his throat. He downed a couple of extra-strength Tylenol with coffee instead.

Twenty minutes later, Craig returned to Kim's place and softly knocked. Kim was still out. After looking around nervously, Craig opened the door and saw Bao unconscious on the floor, lips hanging open, a quizzical wrinkle on his forehead. Craig went in and rummaged for valuables. After throwing Kim's clothes on the floor and opening all the drawers, he left with a leather jacket, a laptop, and a fancy-looking pair of Nikes. Then he returned to Kim's, wrapped the dog in an old blanket, and carried him down the concrete stairwell to his truck. Craig lay the dog in the back seat and headed out to the swamp in the nearby Everglades, about eighteen miles away. He had visited it a few times since he'd seen it in the news a couple of years ago. It was typically a busy tourist spot but not during the pandemic. Craig set Bao down at the edge of the water. The dog did not stir. Craig backed past the Warning sign he'd seen on every visit and drove home as quickly as he could.

He was about to head upstairs when he noticed a camera outside the access door to the garage. "Dammit!" he muttered. A glaring giveaway. *A lawsuit or jail...* That wasn't the outcome he wanted. Homelessness, if he was lucky. But where would *he* move? He was jobless in a pandemic—no one would take him. He hopped into his truck again and sped back to the swamp, desperate to retrieve the dog. But Bao was not where he'd left him. "Bao!" Craig called out. He crept along the edge of the swamp, peering around gnarled tree roots that jutted out from the thick undergrowth. A sudden pain ripped through his leg as something dragged him in. "Fuck!" he cried out faintly. There was some thrashing around the water for a few seconds, then stillness. Somewhere deep in the woods beyond, an animal started howling.

Later that day, Kim came home and found his apartment in a mess, the door wide open. He thought of Craig for a second, then decided he'd confront the racist bastard in the morning. After he called the police, he made his way to the super's, swearing angrily, regretful that he'd moved into the building just to save thirty dollars a month. Kim asked to check the security cameras to see what might have happened, but none of the viewcams revealed anything. The only unexamined camera—the one by the garage door—was broken. The service appointment had been cancelled and postponed indefinitely due to COVID-19.

AGAPE

DANIELA VIOLIN

He wants agape love. Just love from God, and I am learning what that means. So even though I could love him from the depths of me, I will leave him free. I want to be free as well, despite my condition. I just started walking at home again, so it shouldn't be long. That damn fall left me in a wheelchair; it's been more than a year!

His cancer is gone, his teeth fixed, he has places to go and things to do, and so do I. We can go together and apart and together and apart, like dolphins, like fish in the sea. I stand by him, as the family he chooses, while he reconnects with the rest of the family he created. Other people are gaping at a man who would rather say "143" for "I love you" and knows the first hundred numbers to pi. I listen to the music he plays and I know what he wants from me. He wants to be a universal soldier playing foreigner for a beautiful girl—the beautiful girl is me.

THE DAMN POEM

LAUREL SCHELL

I don't want your lungs anymore
I didn't ever really want them
But you offered them up when
You saw my lips turn blue
As I gasped my confession
Of fathomless love for you

And I don't blame you for
Suddenly taking them back
They're yours after all
You need them to breathe

Taking them back
And leaving me there
Sharing my own with my mother
Like a Frida Kahlo painting
All blood and organs, crude
Surgical tools and I don't know

Where I end and she begins
With my head on her breast
I exhale and she inhales sweet
Baby's breath twining
Her life with mine singing
you are my sunshine
my only sunshine

You left when you realized
You couldn't save me
And that I almost killed you

The Damn Poem (continued)

....

Bloody and blinking in
The lights, having saved
Ourselves today we won't
Hang ourselves tomorrow

With our weathered lungs
Expanding in our chests
We inhale and exhale a lifetime.

I need you to know
How many times
You saved my life—
Not with your lungs
But your love.

TEN THINGS I LEARNED ABOUT ANGELA

PUJA MALANI

....

1. She *loves* purple: purple clothes, pillows, sheets, duvets, walls, boots, even purple lipstick.

2. She has an uncanny gift for recognizing different aspects of shades of colours and what each entails.

3. She says men choose her. She's never really chosen a man.

4. She dresses in feminine styles and colours that dazzle.

5. She says only certain men choose her because of her weight.

6. She is brilliant about IT accessibility and how to address people's varied challenges.

7. She is easy to talk with about men and sex. We could talk for hours on end, and we do.

8. She is excellent at saving money, and at a young age bought herself a beautiful house.

9. She hates "white privilege"—she says she had to work extremely hard to get where she is, unlike "them."

10. She is beginning to discover and accept her beautiful, brilliant true self and the many gifts she can offer the world.

....

TRAVELLING 101

SHEREL PURCELL

....

"I'm from the North—a law student." At first glance, Joe seemed quite ordinary, with a pale moon face and grey eyes that didn't reveal much, framed by close-cropped, mouse-coloured hair.

I'd just arrived in Dublin—home of my favourite literary characters and their creators, along with the private language school in the city centre where I'd be teaching English, for half what I'd earn in Toronto, to whiny European kids who'd rather be elsewhere.

I was twenty-four, and it was my first big trip away from home. And although I was nervous—a condition I'd inherited from my anxious mother, who'd seemed overly concerned for my safety and dead set against the trip—I thought it important to expand my horizons so as not to live in fear. My wavering voice, though, did little to dispel Mom's trepidations, as evidenced by her agitated nail-picking as I was packing.

On my first morning in Dublin, as I shopped the thrift stores for work clothes, a man in a dusty overcoat snatched my bag, which contained my cash and passport. My credit card, to the relief of my new landlady (who'd been reluctant to accept it), was back at her bed and breakfast near St. Stephen's Green. She contacted the Gardaí—the Irish police—who didn't believe I'd ever see my bag again. I felt as though I'd failed Travelling 101.

"You're not terribly lucky, are you?" The landlady regarded me suspiciously and seemed relieved when I moved on to longer-term accommodations in a shared house: a large, gloomy Georgian at the end of a cul-de-sac and a fifteen-minute cycle to work.

Still shaken, and fearing Mom might have been right after all, I headed to the safety of my second-floor room, secluded at the top of a long staircase. It was spacious but dark, with one small window, faded rose wallpaper, and threadbare carpeting. Its one redeeming feature, the peat fireplace, proved necessary against the chill, damp Irish evenings.

....

My five roommates included Sue, a Haight-Ashbury artist in her forties obsessed with Celtic crosses, three medical students—two Irish and a Brit—and Joe.

Joe spent all day locked in his room, venturing out only at dinnertime to recite snippets of the daily news, with a focus on the evildoings of the Americans and Brits—a bit awkward as we had one of each in the house. They in turn responded with snickers and questions regarding his sanity. I hated their behaviour.

A Canadian, I avoided Joe's wrath. He greeted me at the door most evenings, beer in hand, in mid-rant, his voice growing more animated as he detailed military tactics, the intricacies of the AK-47, or the destructive capabilities of various nuclear weapons, which he knew intimately, as beloved as family members. I tried steering the conversation to lighter topics with little success, though he would reward me occasionally with a brief smile.

It was 1986, thirteen years before the end of Ireland's "Troubles"—the violent sectarian struggle in Northern Ireland whereby the Protestant majority fought the Irish Republicans' demands for a united Ireland, while divesting the economically disadvantaged Catholic minority of equal rights.

Joe, a Catholic Northerner, would understandably be upset over politics, but I suspected he was dealing with personal problems that the others couldn't see, and despite my pleas for compassion, they continued to goad and tease him about his rants. I'd developed a sensitivity to people like Joe from a childhood fondness for my schizophrenic grandfather—a kind, quiet, and gentle man who my grandmother would harshly berate for his dreamy states, "foolish talk," and frequent, abrupt departures from noisy family gatherings.

Arriving home one Friday night, a month into my stay and soaked from cycling through the perpetual Irish mist, I was grateful for a quiet house.

....

"Where's everyone?" Fighting fever and chills, I turned on the gas burner under the ancient tea kettle.

"Gone for the weekend." Sue glanced up from her Celtic-cross drawings. "Except your boyfriend." She rolled her eyes toward the little room off the kitchen. "And he's even weirder than usual—pacing and muttering to himself, going on about the end of the world."

Thankfully, the hissing kettle cut her short. Upstairs, I made a fire, popped three aspirins, downed a hot whisky, and passed out.

Sue's knock woke me. The wind and rain were beating against the darkened window.

"He's down there barricading the place, pushing furniture against the doors and windows and ranting about some war."

I raised myself on one arm, too tired and sick to care. How could Sue, an artist, be so insensitive when it came to the plight of others? "Throw another brick on the fire, then get a drink and sit here."

As if on cue, the lights went out.

"It's the storm." The reassurance slipped from my voice as footsteps approached and paused just outside the door. "Joe? What happened to the lights? Is it the storm? Come in and have a drink."

Sue elbowed me. The door opened. As Joe moved into the room, his shadow, cast by the firelight, grew larger over the walls and ceiling. I glanced up at his face. Joe had disappeared.

"I think someone's here." His voice was dead, like someone talking in their sleep. "Someone who shouldn't be."

No kidding. "You think someone's breaking in?" My singsongy, little kid's voice annoyed me, but I felt that playing naive might save all of us.

"Could be."

"I'll go get the police."

"Right," he said. "Get the Gardaí. It's time for you to go."

I was right, my innocent tone seemed to placate him. He wouldn't hurt me. I remembered our after-work chats and was grateful for the little efforts I'd made to listen to him, wishing I'd been able to convince the others to do likewise.

"But she stays." He turned to Sue. "She's been a bad girl."

Something died in her throat, and I felt Sue slump deeper into the mattress. I handed him the bottle. "Go down and fix some drinks while I get ready."

We remained frozen on the bed until we heard his last footfall on the stairs, then scrambled into jackets and sweaters. Sue's feet barely fit into my sneakers. In total darkness we inched down the stairs, hugging the wall. I was in the lead, trying to block Sue behind me. Some inner resolve had kicked in. I would get us out of there.

The street light illuminated a large pile of furniture stacked against the living room window and the front door, with the exception of a twelve-inch opening that Joe was guarding with a raised shovel. I approached the door, pretending Sue wasn't attached to me and Joe wasn't holding a weapon.

"She's not going," he said.

"It's dark. I'm scared to go alone." I pulled her arm after me through the opening.

He grabbed the other.

I stared into his vacant eyes, speaking calmly, resolutely. "It's not going to work, Joe."

He loosened his grip for a second and, with a final pull of Sue's arm, we were outside, running down the street through the wind and rain to the corner store. An hour later, escorted by two Gardaí, we returned to the house. Joe had vanished.

One of the officers whistled as he inspected his handiwork. "Yer man meant business. You were lucky."

EXCERPTS FROM *KISMET*

MAYA AMEYAW

....

PROLOGUE

"Are you ready?"

"Always." I complete one final stretch, bending my left leg at an angle most would find impossible.

Neil smiles as I shake out my legs and bounce *en pointe* a few times.

Then we're being motioned to take our places onstage.

We settle into our starting positions, facing each other. As the lighting dims, I watch him transform. His eyes darken, all of their usual humour leaving them. Instinct is all that remains.

The same change is happening in me as our first note plays.

I forget about all the important people watching us and disengage from myself. Neil and I are now nothing but our movements, endlessly fluid and in sync.

When the music's over, we bow as one. Before I even look up, I hear it, like an unexpected rainstorm. The thunderous crack of hundreds of pairs of palms pounding against each other. The audience are on their feet, and instead of the noise winding down, it seems to build momentum.

I turn to Neil and I'm sure his look of stunned disbelief mirrors my own.

Then he's grinning. He picks me up and I'm laughing as the lights overhead blind me, the world reduced to a shimmering white haze.

....

CHAPTER 1

My discomfort is like an itchy wool blanket shrouding the doctor's large sunlit office. It weighs me down and begins to smother me, slowly sucking the air out of the room.

I can see him silently appraising me, but not in the way I'm used to when my instructors examine the lines my body creates. Instead, he is appraising my mind.

This is my fourth time seeing him. The fourth time I feel a disconnect so wide we may as well be in different rooms.

The only sound is his pen tapping against my closed file as we stare at each other. Everything he knows about me comes from that file. He knows my parents divorced two months ago. He knows I'm five-foot-nine and my weight is only in the double digits. He knows I passed out during practice twice last week. He knows how long I will have to stay in this awful place filled with girls slowly trying to disappear.

"The sooner you open up, the sooner you'll get out of here," he says in a way he must think will make him appear genuine and sincere. "You're doing well with putting weight back on, so talking about it is the only thing stopping you from getting back to your life."

I continue looking at him blandly as I fiddle with the friendship bracelet Neil gave me last year for my fourteenth birthday, a week before we won our first competition together. The braided rainbow band is frayed and hangs dangerously loose on my wrist. I imagine tearing it off. He promised to trust me when I said I had everything under control.

. . . .

The urge to jump out of my seat is so strong, I wrap my fingers around the armrest. I need to get out of here. I need to be moving, out of my head, away from my thoughts and into my body.

My body. The thing everyone is so obsessed with. The doctors here, weighing me every day. And my mother before that, weighing me every week, taking my measurements, monitoring every bite of food. But no matter what she did, my body disobeyed her. Growing taller than all the other girls I danced with, my stick-straight figure beginning to curve. Slowly destroying her dreams for my ballet career.

I grip the armrest harder. I can't be here anymore. "My mother doesn't let me eat as much when I'm training."

He looks pleased with himself. Like he's made a breakthrough, built some trust with a troubled teen. The truth is, I can't even remember what he said his name was. I just need to be back in the studio. I've already missed a week of training.

He writes it all down and I feel like he's embarrassed for me when he figures out how powerless I am, that I just let her do this to me. But this is how it's always been with my mother and me. I do what she tells me to.

He probably wonders why I didn't rebel against her like a normal teenager, but he doesn't ask. There is no normal for me. There is dance, and I don't know what I am without that.

. . . .

COMING HOME FROM DEATH—
MEETING LIFE WITH SPIRIT: A MEMOIR

ROMAINE JONES

We always held hands while I visited him each day in Bridgepoint Palliative Care Hospice. Guy lay propped up in his curtained-off bed space in an airy and brightly lit double room. Idyllically, through a full-sized window, he faced the snowy hills of quiet, spacious Withrow Park. But Guy's frailty from brain cancer prevented him from walking at all. He'd surely have cherished the view.

That day, Guy's sniffling oxygen tank sprays blue bubbles into his nostrils. His gasping and gurgling throat tries to compete, his neck compulsively twisting from side to side. His heavy eyelids hovers, almost closed, probably from exhaustion.

Two young nurses call, "His oxygen is diminishing."

"Yes," I whisper, "I see. It's low…"

Guy's shuddering lessens. The machine sniffles to itself alone, with a groan, imitating inconsolable weeping.

Staff and visitors tiptoe in, whisper solace, patting his shoulder, stroking and squeezing his hand, urging, "Keep going! We're with you!"

Each soul sighs and leaves.

A chilled draft startles me, entering as though someone or something is listening, turning up the volume—of what? An odd atmosphere settles in, and the mood in the room shifts. A strong, positive force waits, watches in silence—fine-tuning with instinct, as though waiting for a show to begin. Or a performance we must initiate: to see or hear, witness or challenge. Anticipation nudges. Prepare. This performance depends on us, on Guy and me. It is now due. We are in the hands of *us*. We are in our *own hands*.

What have we got to lose?

The new feel of our suite inspires me. I find myself lowering his left side bars, sliding my right arm around his shoulders. I cup his arms with energy and ease, one hand around his once-upon-a-time thick and

....

wavy head of silver hair—so beautiful before his six-week chemo and radiation treatments at Sunnybrook Hospital.

Murmuring sweet nothings as ever before, I delight in holding, cuddling, and caressing my beloved. All of this brings to mind our earlier "best time ever" intimacies, when we could savour our good health—pre-cancer years, when our lives bloomed and flourished.

Musing on Guy's grim weakness that day, on a sudden impulse I wondered how damaged his eyes were. Probably in bad shape, I surmised, but here goes. Reaching over, I gently pressed my thumb to his eyelid. And to my astonishment, I was completely shocked! His beautiful green eye beamed radiantly at me! Guy, too, looked just as shocked as I! I screamed with joy.

Again and again, this deep green, round, moonlike eye gazed at me—with recognition! It hypnotized me!

Imagine a moon in its fullness, surprising me—as though I were actually lying beside the moon, a moon so full, floating on a pearl-white globe: gorgeous.

I yelped with thankfulness, "You're there! Your eye is alive! I can see you—can you see me, my love?"

A strange but familiar voice message conveyed *Yes* without a word or a gesture: I could hear it in my mind.

His intense listening stunned me and made him stronger. He knew he was home.

Guy's diminishing breath and air slowly shut down. Yet he held me, conveying a strength he'd never shown before. I'd never felt such a strong bond with him—until the end. In that short earth time together, I was swept away in the moment of having heard a sudden, soft patter of light, a miniature patter of tiny feet in a close and unfamiliar passage. The cluster of unknown beings fluttered around us, flying just beyond

....

us, whirring: a fairy-like flock of angel wings, sweeping through the corridor. Their voices twinkled as they flew and flashed quickly by.

Guy let me join him as he slipped over the Border between Life and Death. Through Eternity. Infinity expanded in size, depth, and space as he passed that Border. He emanated love as he passed. An unstoppable express train appeared to us.

We conveyed our eternal embrace. He emanated that we wipe out all regrets we'd had with each other and any harm we may have caused one another.

We became one soul, heart and spirit. We became Home to each other.

DYING

EMILY GILLESPIE

My name is Emily.
I'm a mentally ill artist,
and my dad is dying.

This is how I introduced myself for years.
Dying—palliative, dying—ongoing
but needing something to die from...
Act of dying, never stopping.
Dying as a permanent state of being.

My name is Emily
and my dad died last month.
Dead.
No longer dying,
but he was dying so long
we all thought he'd live forever.

LIBRARY SCRIPT

EMILY GILLESPIE

....

To the medical doctors who think life-saving meds for the mentally ill only come in neat little bottles with stapled prescription receipts, *are you ever wrong.*

When I was a kid without many friends, the local librarian put books aside for me, somehow knowing what stories I needed. Now my heart hurts so much that even CAMH ER can do nothing for me.

Before this breakdown, breakthrough, or whatever this is, I was a one-book-at-a-time kinda mind. But now—now my heart is bleeding so much, one book isn't enough to pack the wound.

My psychiatrist gave me three different anxiety meds: *here's the med I want you on, and here's the med to reduce the anxiety spike from the new med, and here's something for your stomach too.*

My life is kinda like that: here's my heart problem, my life problem, the root of my existential sorrow. And I need to hear the right words, for my survival.

And so, in the stack of books on my battered coffee table is a volume on mad people's history, showing me I'm not the only one who's been cast out of society and viewed as useless, reminding me that my life is shaped by trends in psychiatric treatment. Mad people's history whispers to me: it's okay, you have a right to be here, please stay a little longer, for those of us who didn't make it... Page after page about forms of torture, and when I think I've heard the worst, well, there's still one more page...

....

With Queen Street under construction, I run my hand along the wall that past inmates built, and I know that if I'm just a speck in history, I'm definitely part of mad people's history.

Then I ask myself, *what do I need next?* And the answer is *hope*.

Hope that I'm part of something bigger than myself, as I nestle in bed, with my weighted blanket and stuffed animals, my mug of tea, and the best of my queer poetry collection. I flip through questions about identity and prayers to the stars, and suddenly my sorrow is more than just mine.

And then, when the poets tuck me into bed for the night, they ask, *what do you need now?* What do I need, I repeat, as the sleeping pills muddle my mind, and I am finally relaxed enough to let go of the tension in my back, my jaw, as I lie in my soft bed of pillows and unicorn stuffies.

What I need is space, not only to live, but to dream of a world where I can exist as I am, where I am not just getting by, but celebrated, loved. I want to sleep forever—but wait: no, that's not quite it, I want to be able to sleep and wake and dream of a better world.

And then I open a book on disability justice, and it talks of surviving the apocalypse and of prefigurative politics, which is about imagining and dreaming of the world we want, we need, living as if we are already there.

And so I dream of a nice long street where all my mad artist friends are neighbours and we share our skills and sorrows and I'm never alone and the ocean bookmarks our road.

At last, with all my meds, and with all my wild survival dreams, I sleep.

THE COVER ARTIST

....

APANAKI TEMITAYO M is a Toronto-based multidisciplinary, multimedia fibre artist and art facilitator. Her work—which includes materials such as African fabrics, cowrie shells, and alcohol ink—reflects on a diverse range of topics, including spirituality, Black womanhood, mental health, and Afrofuturism. Apanaki is the first Artist-in-Wellness for CAMH and was the 2017–18 Workman Arts Artist-in-Residence. She is an art facilitator for the Workman Arts Art-Cart Program and her work has been featured in Toronto and abroad at the Amazing Nina Simone Documentary Exhibition (NYC), the African American Fiber Art Exhibit (North Carolina), and the Growing Room Feminist Literary Festival (Vancouver).

This piece is called Oju Olorun I: Eye of God I, *from the collection of the same name. The collection was inspired by images of rock formations in the Antelope Canyon on Navajo land near Page, Arizona. The collection is a symbolization of the combination of the sky against the rock formations, which to me is nature's rendering of the god self. Hence also, the name* Oju Olorun, *which is Yoruba for* Eye of God *to connect Turtle Island Indigeneity and African Indigeneity.*

ABOUT THE CONTRIBUTORS

....

MAYA AMEYAW is a freelance writer and peer support facilitator at CMHA Toronto, where she supports InkWell Workshops. Previously, she helped curate and contributed to the mental-health anthologies *A Place for Us*, *The Double World*, *The Unexpected Sky*, and *I Am a Lake*. Maya is working on her first novel, *Kismet*, about high school students struggling with trauma and mental health issues, with funding from the Toronto Arts Council and Ontario Arts Council.

MICHELE BRETON enjoys listening to poetry slams and spoken-word performances and reading. For several years, her main love has been writing her own poetry and short stories. She has been published in four zines and three previous InkWell anthologies.

REBECCA CHERNECKI has been part of the Bruised Years Choir at Workman Arts since 2017. Her poetry has been published in a chapbook called *Poetry from Our Peaceful Place*, with Michael Garron Hospital, and her artwork has been sold at VanDuzer Art Studio and with Being Scene at the Gladstone Hotel. She holds a B.A. in political science from the University of Western Ontario and nearly completed a Master's in Women's Studies from OISE at the University of Toronto. She struggles with issues in her life related to trauma and likes to make soup.

PAMELA CHYNN has been a proud InkWell participant for over three years. She credits InkWell with giving her the inspiration and courage to pursue her creative writing ambitions, including completing her second creative writing certificate at George Brown College this year.

DONNA COOKE lives and works in Toronto with her husband and three boys. She loves to write, travel, and hike and enjoys reading young adult fiction, mysteries, and creative non-fiction.

....

EUNICE CU is launching a second career as a writer and freelance editor after practising as a clinical pharmacist in her homeland of New Zealand. When it comes to life, she has more questions than answers but finds that writing and surrounding herself with people in the same boat helps her figure it out.

LORETTA FISHER writes voraciously with a view to making core ideas and current events clear. Check out her byline in *Spring Magazine* championing workers' rights and social, economic, racial, and climate justice. Editorializing poetically is her passion. With a team or flying solo, she writes from authentic experience, exposing unfair barriers and revealing our true connections.

EMILY GILLESPIE is an author, activist, and daydreamer. She has an M.A. in disability studies. *Dancing with Ghosts* (2017) is her first novel. She is currently working on her second book. Her writing appears in several anthologies.

MARK HARVEY has travelled to many countries, including Australia. He was a student at the University of Toronto, where he was an English major and wrote for several campus newspapers. He also has an extensive acting background. Mark recently graduated from Seneca College's Library & Information Technician program.

NORIKO HOSHINO was born and raised in Tokyo, Japan. She came to Canada in 1997 and now lives in Toronto. Her short story "Spring Snow" won the University of Toronto's Penguin Random House Canada Student Award for Fiction 2017.

FATHUMA JAMA is a diasporic Somali writer/poet living in Toronto. She has been a member of InkWell since 2018.

ROMAINE JONES has been a peace and social-justice activist since the era of H-bomb testing and the American civil rights movement. She is a passionate admirer of Russian authors, particularly memoirist

Nadezhda Mandelstam and her husband, Osip Mandelstam, poet extraordinaire. Romaine is grateful for the generous support of InkWell Workshops.

ASPI KOOTAR was born in Bombay, India. He went to a Jesuit school, where he was introduced to Panaroma poems and Shakespearean plays. An engineer by training, Aspi's love for the English language and poetry continues through InkWell with its fantastic instructors.

ASUKA LAPIERRE is a recent university graduate trying to find her way in a new adult world. Writing for as long as she can remember, she does so to make people feel less alone. She is also a social media specialist for InkWell Workshops.

PUJA MALANI was born in India and has lived in Toronto since the age of four. Much of her writing comes from feeling caught between two cultures and the adventures she's experienced leading a double life. Puja has experienced depression and anxiety since university. Her goal now is to leave a legacy of love and generosity and to inspire others by following all her passions.

YASAMAN MANSOORI is a full-time thinker and freelance doer. She is interested in the iterations of dysfunctional relationships in the modern world. Yasaman is a McGill graduate and former corporate sad girl. She is working on a slightly absurd podcast and is currently a student.

KOSHALA NALLANAYAGAM survives as best as she can with mental and physical illnesses. She worked for many decades as a community health worker in the non-profit sector in Toronto and was active in anti-oppression struggles.

HONEY NOVICK is a singer/songwriter/voice teacher/poet. She facilitates the Voice Yoga program at the Secret Handshake and wrote "I'm Mad— Making a Difference," a tone poem performance piece for the Friendly Spike Theatre Band.

JOSEPH PIRRELLO's writing life officially began when he became an InkWell Workshops member five years ago. Since then, he's been privileged to publish a memoir entitled *Towards Sanity* and a collection of poetry called *Judith's Song*, both available at Indigo stores. Currently, he's working on his second memoir, *Dear Daddy*, and a second collection of poems entitled *Sleep Talk*. InkWell's facilitators have been a main source of inspiration, and he feels greatly indebted to their guidance and insight.

SHEREL PURCELL worked as an editorial assistant for Fitzhenry & Whiteside and now publishes travel pieces on TripSavvy.com, AOL, 10best.com, and in North American newspapers and magazines. She received an editorial award from Parenting Publications of America and scholarships to fiction-writing workshops at the Humber School for Writers and the Maritime Writers' Workshops. Her play *Going Nowhere* was selected for David S. Young's dramaturgical workshop.

DANA SAHADATH (he/him) was diagnosed with a disability at age three and struggled with it for the rest of his childhood. Eventually, he found that embracing his disability made it easier to cope with. He loves being part of InkWell because it gives him an avenue to express himself.

HOWARD J. SANCHEZ has been a workshop participant at InkWell since 2017. Since joining, he has been featured twice in previous InkWell anthologies. He is a first-generation Filipino Canadian from Toronto. With the continuing support he receives through InkWell, he hopes to pursue writing as a full-time career.

LAUREL SCHELL is an actor, writer, and theatre producer. She is trained in physical and devised theatre and has performed on stages across the country. Laurel writes plays, poetry, and creative non-fiction. In addition to her artistic pursuits, she is trained as a birth and post-partum doula.

MG SHEPHERD is much more comfortable writing office memos than attempting creative writing. She has attended InkWell workshops for several years now and, thanks to the fabulous instructors and supportive fellow writers, feels increasingly confident in her writing.

....

DANIELA VIOLIN was first published in 2001, at the age of nineteen, by MacMillan McGraw-Hill, and she has gone on to earn several other publishing credits in New York and California. Although she is Canadian-born and raised, this is her first Canadian publication.

JAMES WAGSTAFF completed a Novel Writing certificate from George Brown College in 2014. He is an avid reader and movie watcher and enjoys going to plays, museums, and art galleries. His favourite author is Terry Brooks.

ADAM ZABOROWSKI lives in Toronto. He has lived experience of mental-health issues and writes on occasion.

GEORGE ZANCOLA is a writer of short stories and poems and is forever trying to write a novel. He is a grateful member of InkWell. He has published his work in *Open Minds Quarterly,* where he won third prize in the 2018 Brainstorm Poetry Contest, the *Humber Literary Review,* the anthology *Not Without Us,* the Friendly Voice, the Hearing Voices Café Newspaper, and two previous InkWell anthologies. In 2018, he was nominated by InkWell Books for the Journey Prize for his short story "The Experiment."

....